Rose Hip Rose 3

Presented by TORU FUJISAWA

Rose Hip Rose Volume 3
Created by Tohru Fujisawa

Translation - Nan Rymer
English Adapation - Michael French
Retouch and Lettering - Star Print Brokers
Production Artist - Vicente Rivera, Jr.
Graphic Designer - Colin Graham

Editor - Hyun Joo Kim
Pre-Production Supervisor - Vicente Rivera, Jr.
Print-Production Specialist - Lucas Rivera
Managing Editor - Vy Nguyen
Senior Designer - Louis Csontos
Senior Designer - James Lee
Senior Editor - Bryce P. Coleman
Senior Editor - Jenna Winterberg
Associate Publisher - Marco F. Pavia
President and C.O.O. - John Parker
C.E.O. and Chief Creative Officer - Stu Levy

A 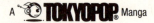 Manga

TOKYOPOP and are trademarks or registered trademarks of TOKYOPOP Inc.

TOKYOPOP Inc.
5900 Wilshire Blvd. Suite 2000
Los Angeles, CA 90036

E-mail: info@TOKYOPOP.com
Come visit us online at www.TOKYOPOP.com

© 2006 Tohru Fujisawa. All Rights Reserved. All rights reserved. No portion of this book may be
First Published in Japan in 2006 by Kodansha Ltd., Tokyo. reproduced or transmitted in any form or by any means
English publication rights arranged through Kodansha Ltd. without written permission from the copyright holders.
This manga is a work of fiction. Any resemblance to
actual events or locales or persons, living or dead, is
entirely coincidental.

ISBN: 978-1-4278-0627-7

First TOKYOPOP printing: November 2008
10 9 8 7 6 5 4 3 2 1
Printed in the USA

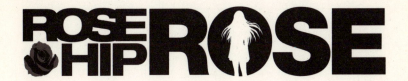

VOLUME 3

by Tohru Fujisawa

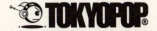

HAMBURG // LONDON // LOS ANGELES // TOKYO

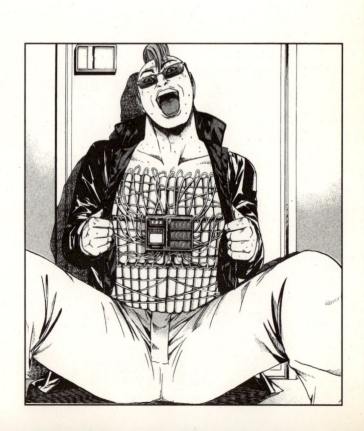

STORY SO FAR...

ROSE HIP ROSE

THE SERIAL KILLER KNOWN AS "SHEPHERD" PLANS TO KILL A 17-YEAR-OLD GIRL NAMED KASUMI ASAKURA. NATSUKI KUONJI, A FORMER ALICE MEMBER, TRANSFERS OVER FROM THE OSAKA POLICE DEPARTMENT TO PROTECT KASUMI. BUT KASUMI IS NO ORDINARY GIRL. SHE ACTUALLY IS PART OF A SPECIAL POLICE TEAM, AND IS FAMOUS FOR HER DEADLY AIM AND USE OF NON-LETHAL WEAPONS. HER CODE NAME: ROSE HIP. IN THE MEANTIME, SHEPHERD'S HENCHMEN KILL MANY INNOCENT PEOPLE AND PLAN TO ATTACK THE CITY HALL IN ORDER TO "CLEANSE" TOKYO. NOW IT IS UP TO ROSE HIP AND NATSUKI--TWO HIGH SCHOOL GIRLS--TO SAVE THE HOSTAGES, THE CITY HALL, AND THEMSELVES.

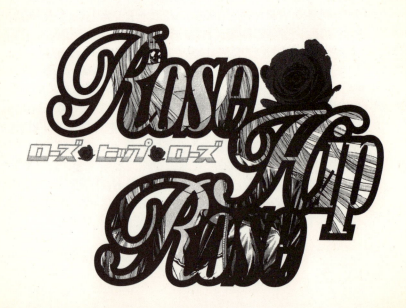

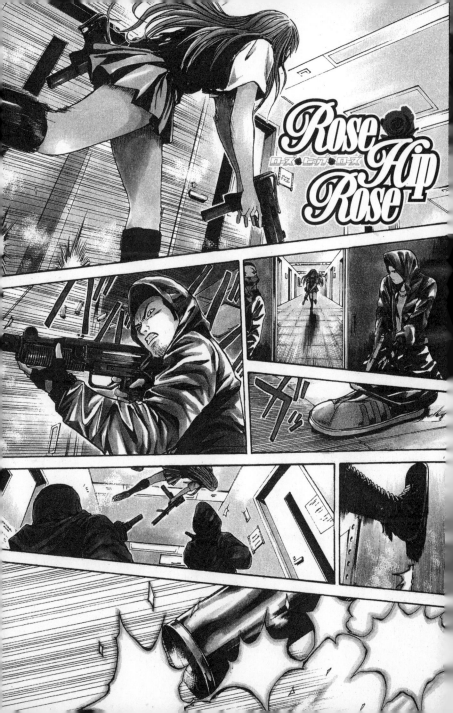

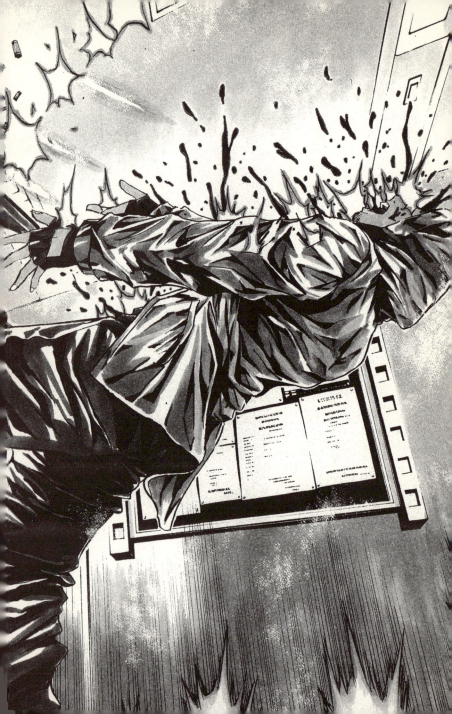

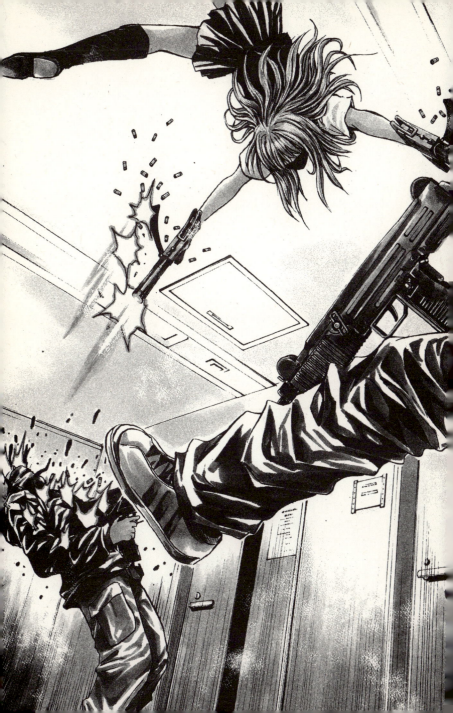

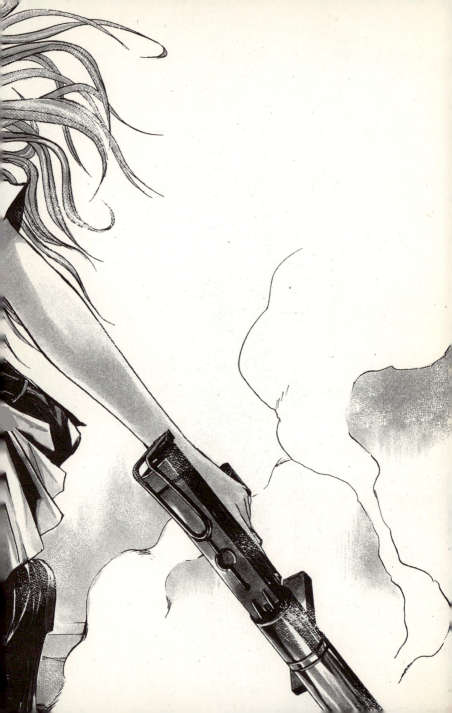

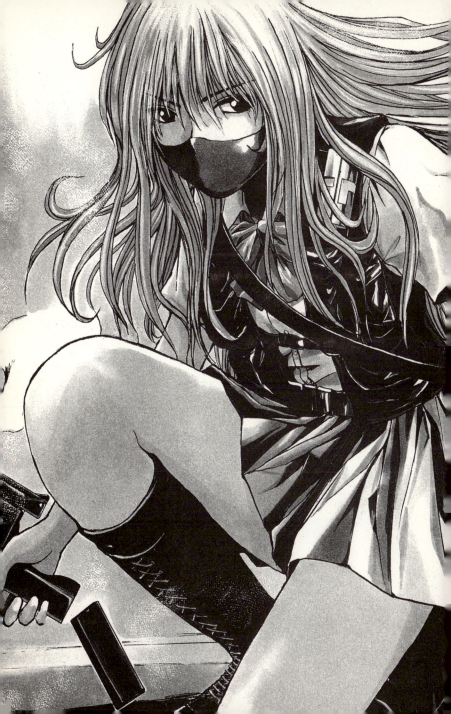

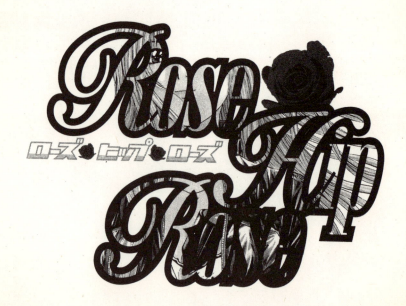

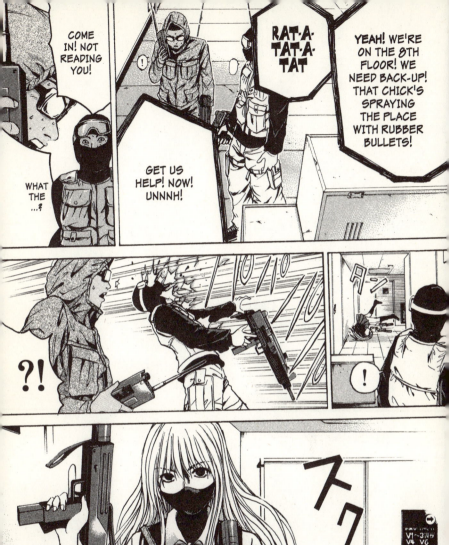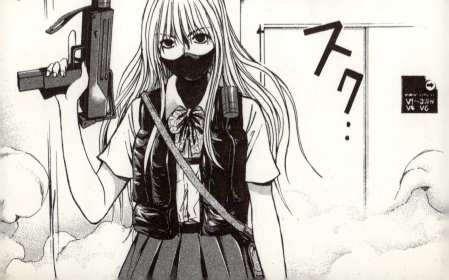

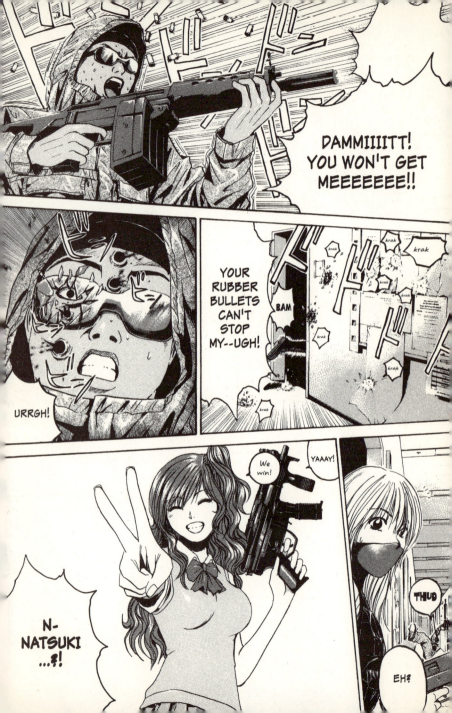

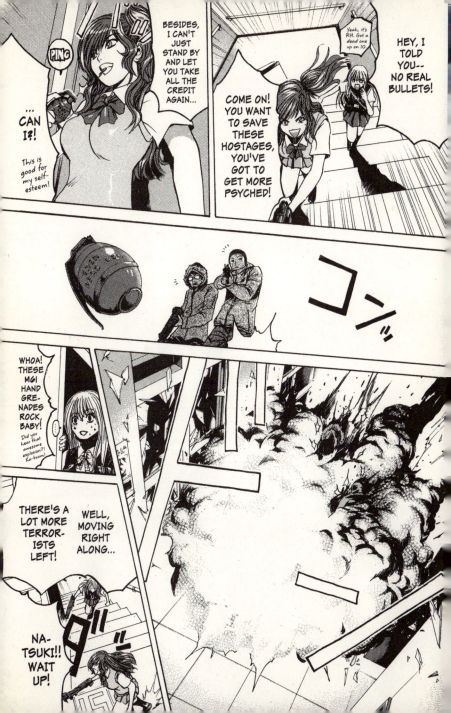

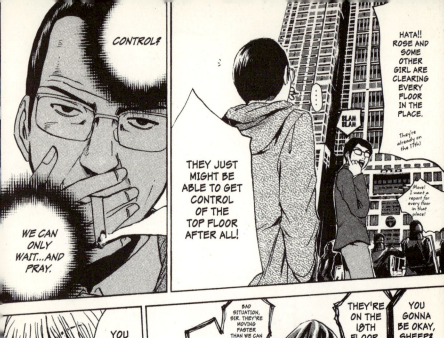
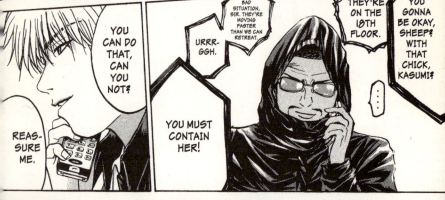
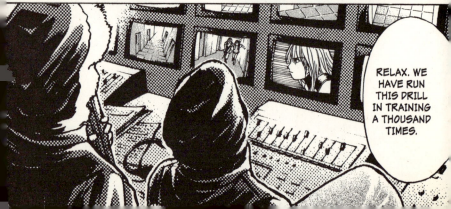

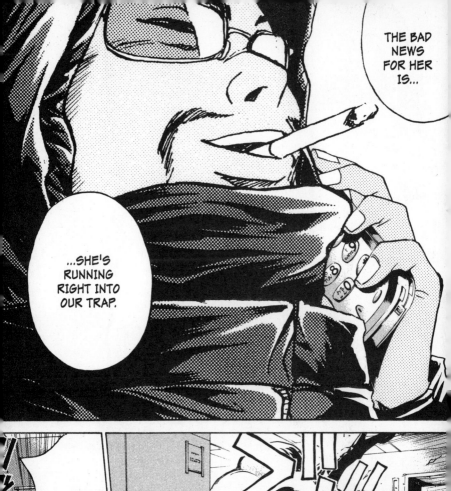
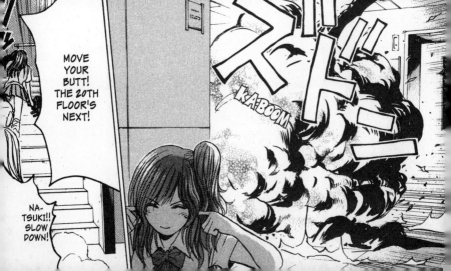

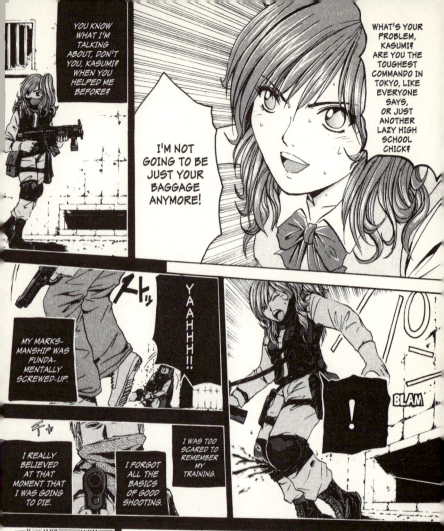

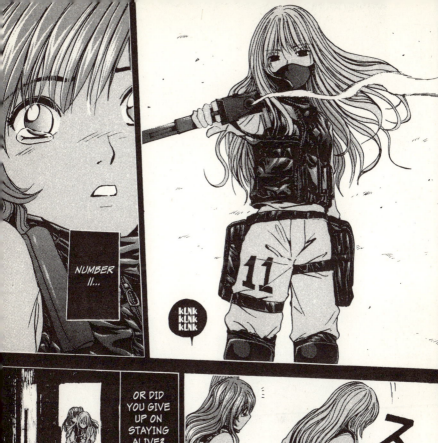

NUMBER 11...

kLNk kLNk kLNk

OR DID YOU GIVE UP ON STAYING ALIVE?

WHY? WHY GIVE UP ON LIFE?

HUH?

WHAT ARE YOU WAITING FOR? MOVE!

AND I'M JUST BAGGAGE FOR ALICE. THERE IS NOTHING I COULD DO TO CHANGE THAT.

BECAUSE I-I'M A COWARD.

IS YOUR LEG HURT?

DON'T THINK THAT. YOUR THOUGHTS CREATE YOUR WORLD, YOU KNOW.

YOU DON'T THINK EVERYONE HERE IS JUST AS SCARED AS YOU?

DO WE LOOK LIKE WE'RE JUST WAITING TO DIE?

WE'RE JUST WORKING TO GET STRONGER.

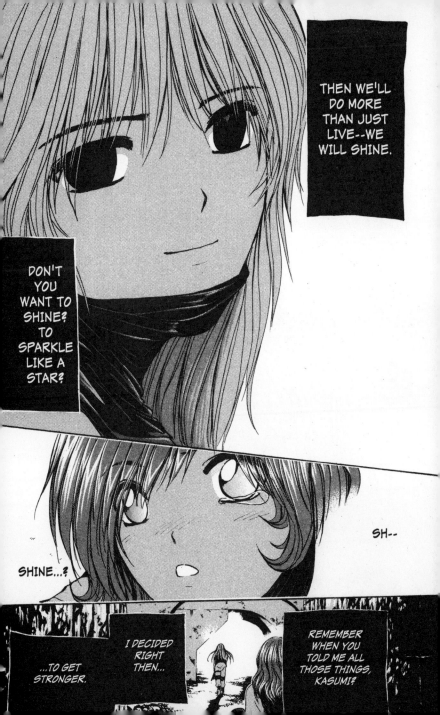

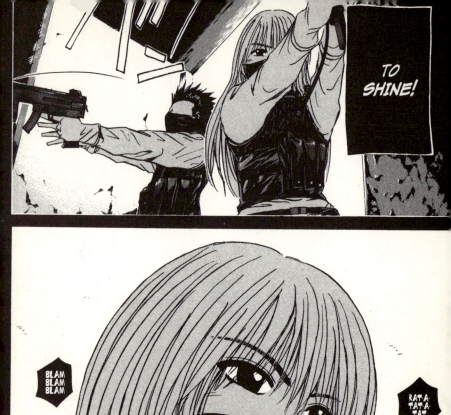
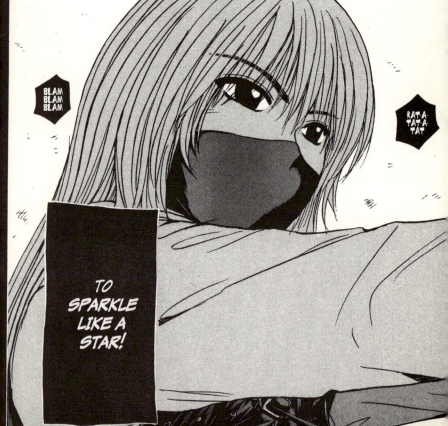

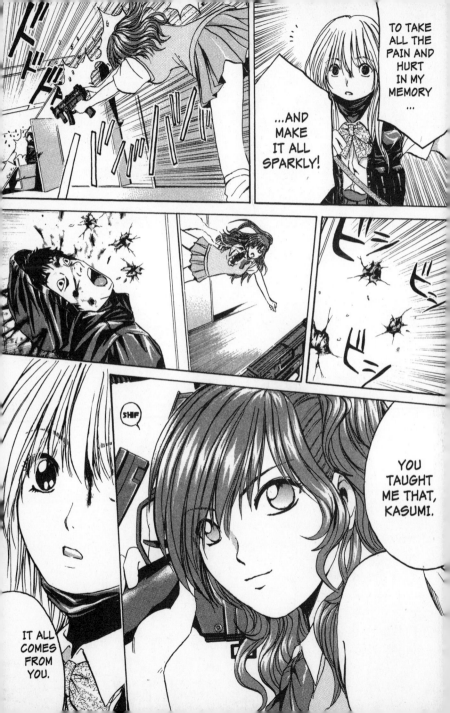

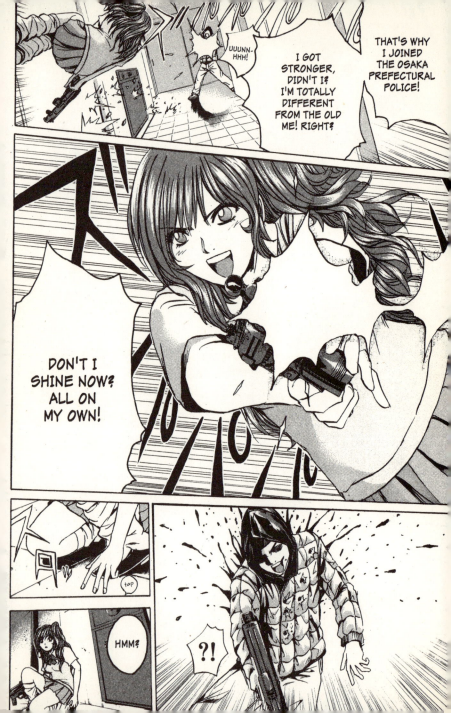

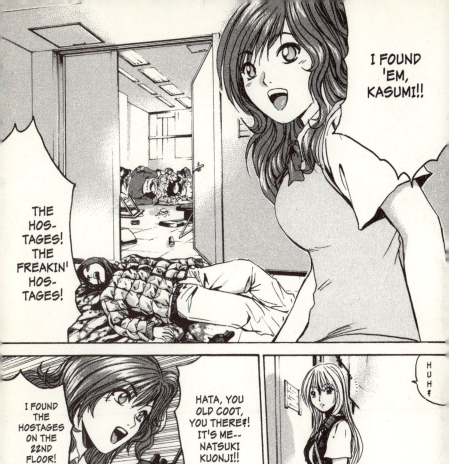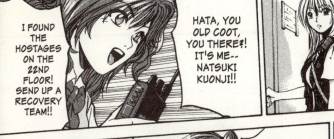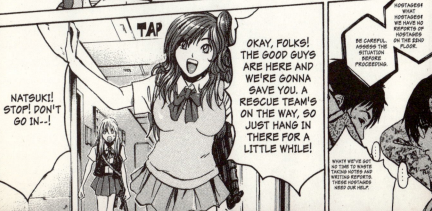

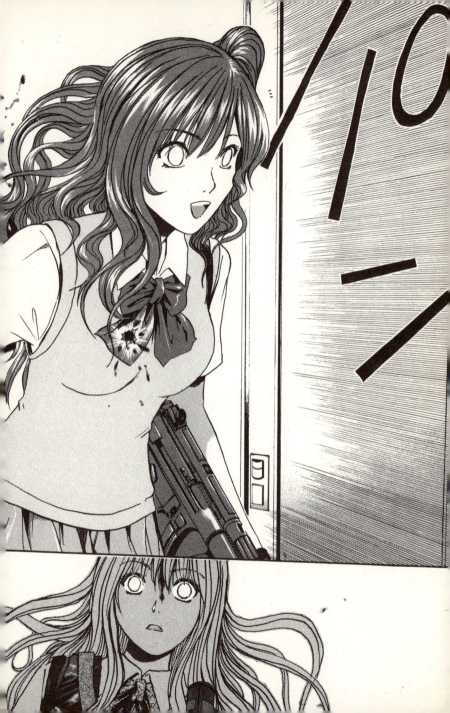

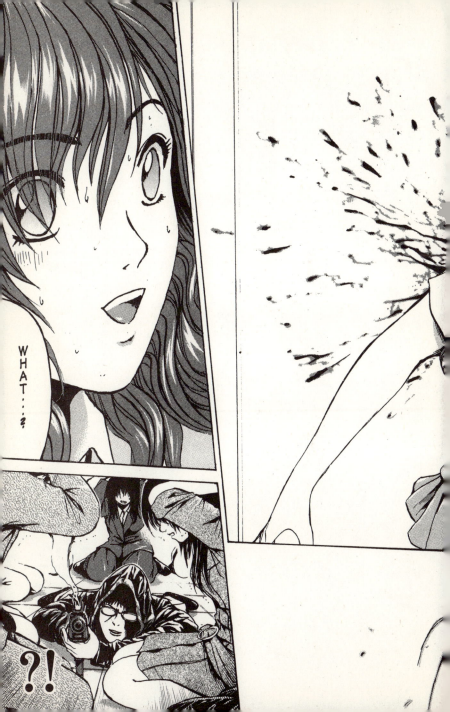

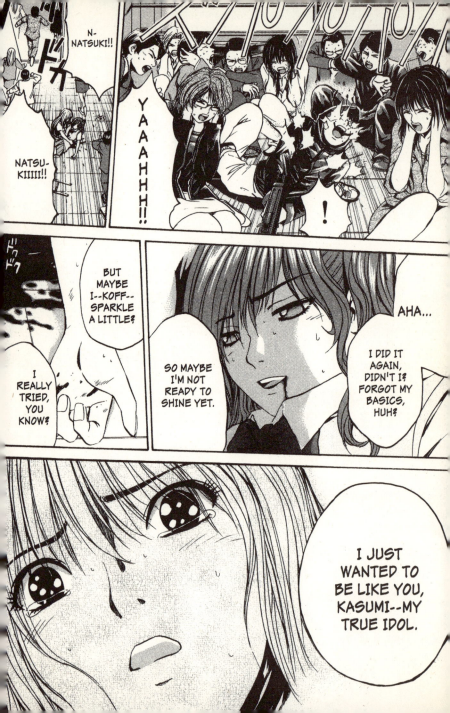

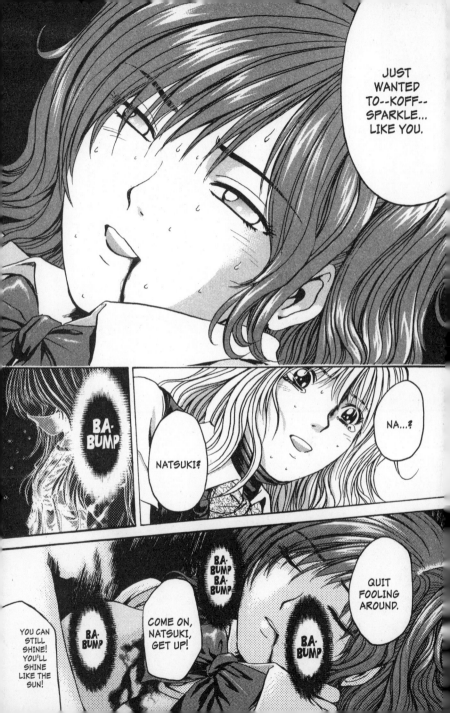

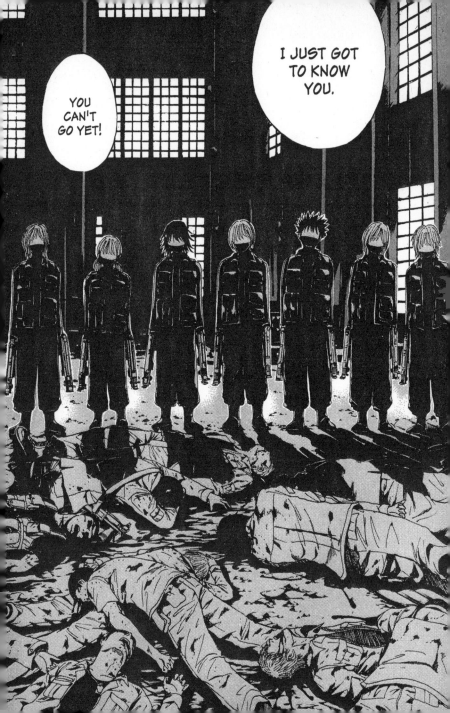

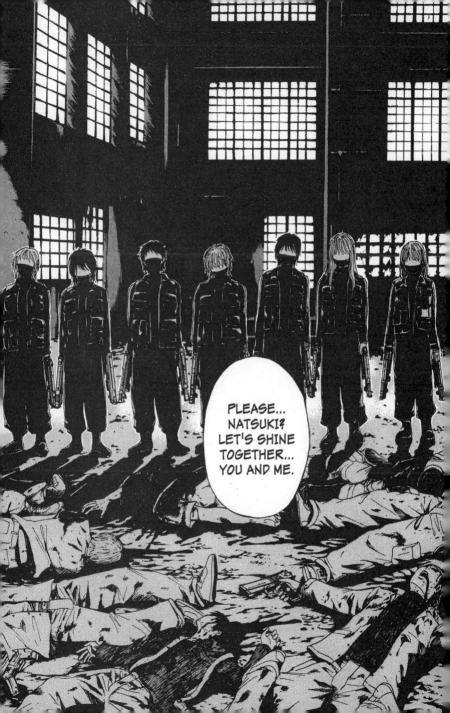

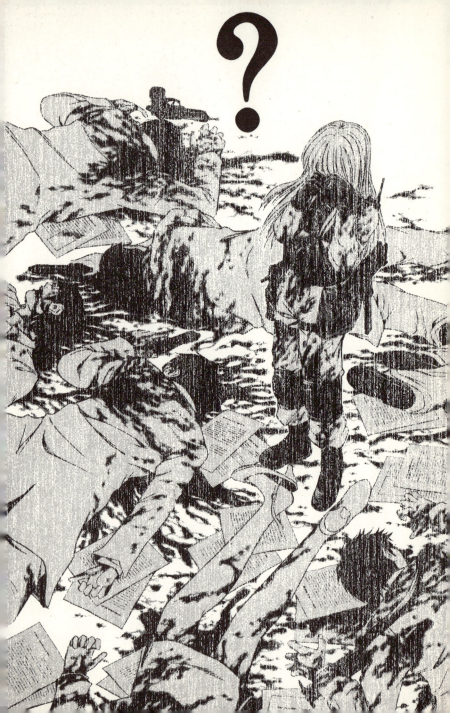

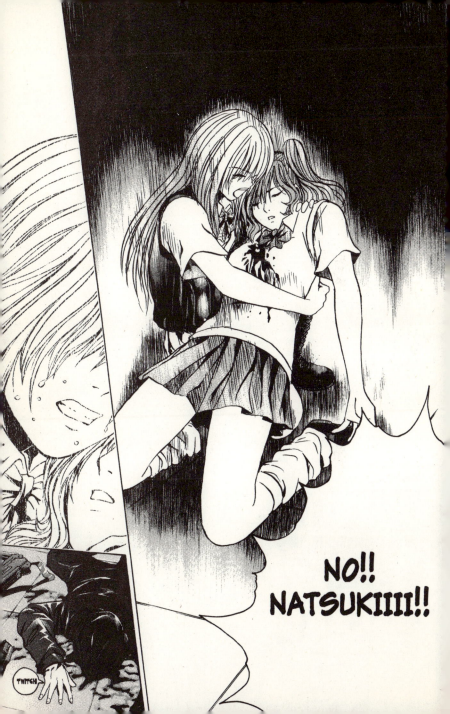

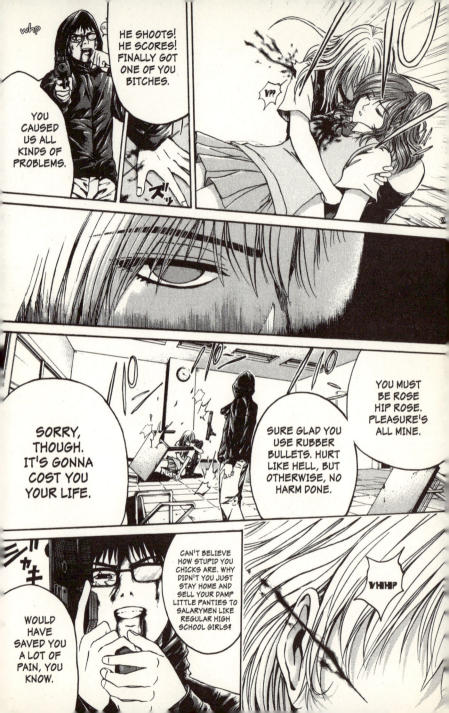

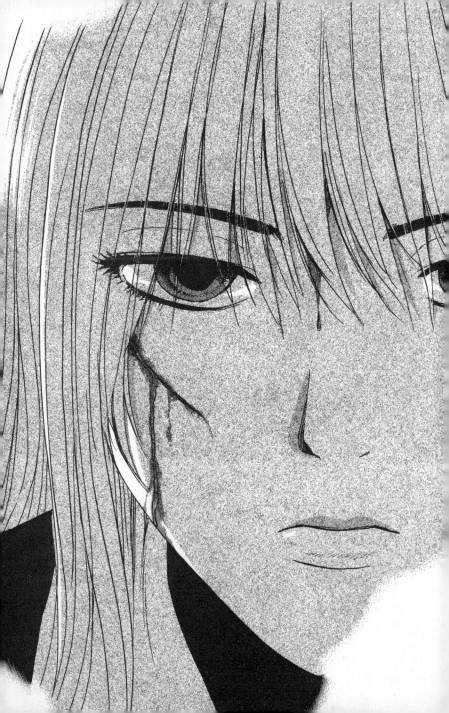

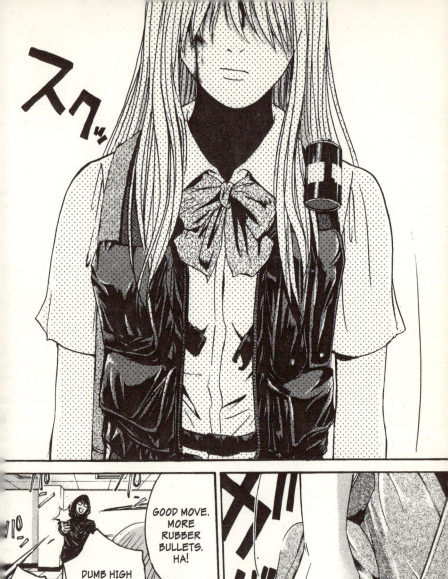
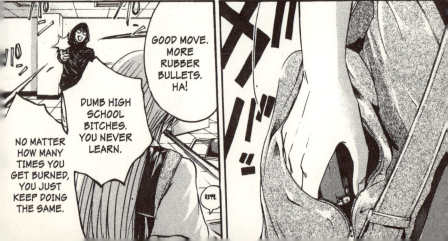

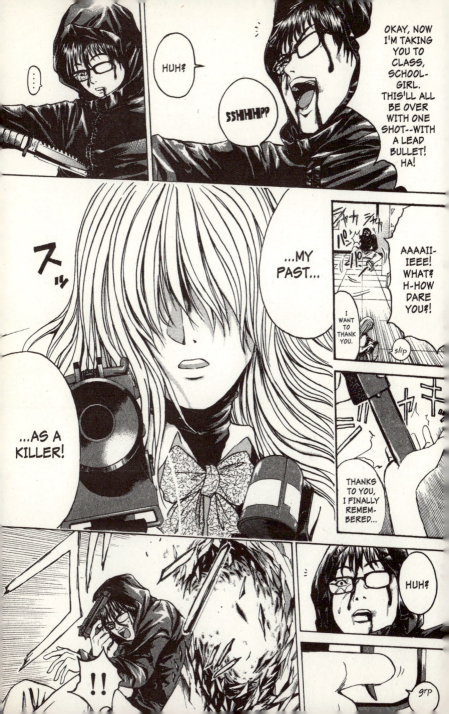

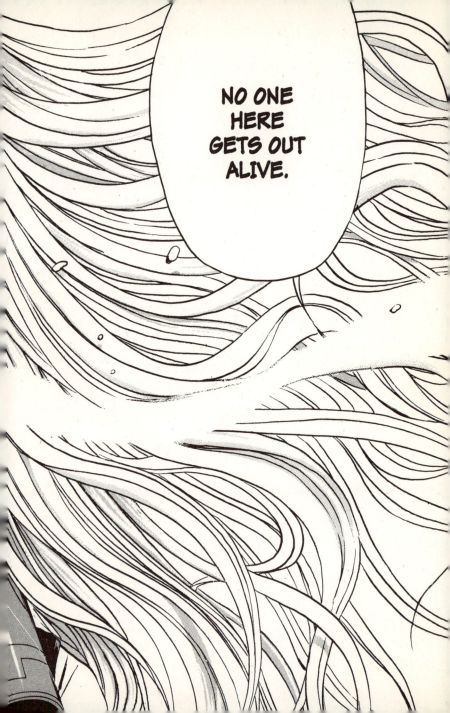

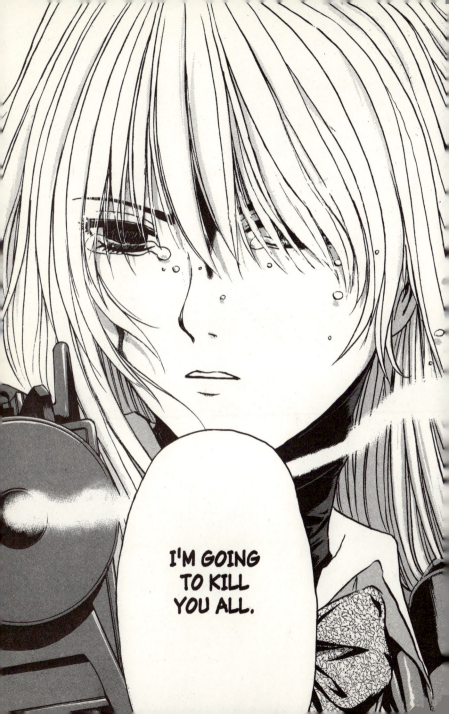

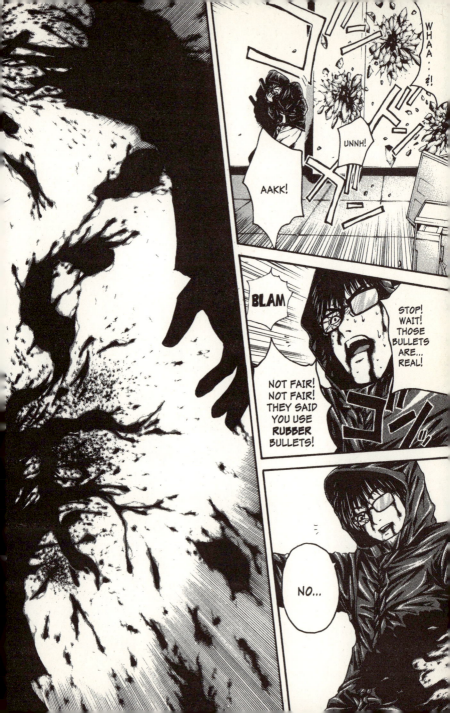

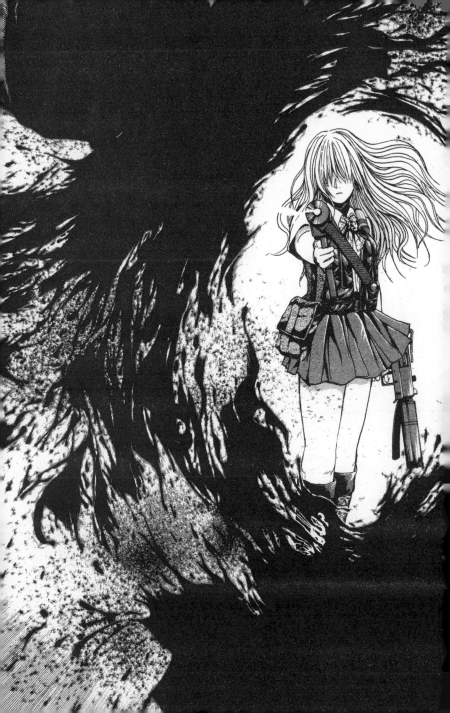

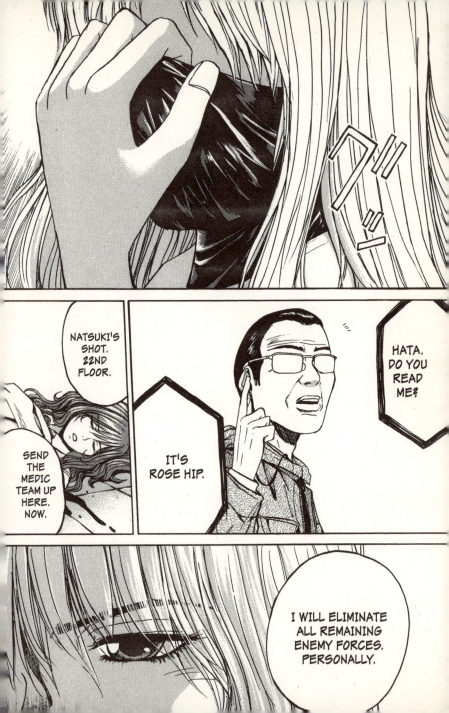

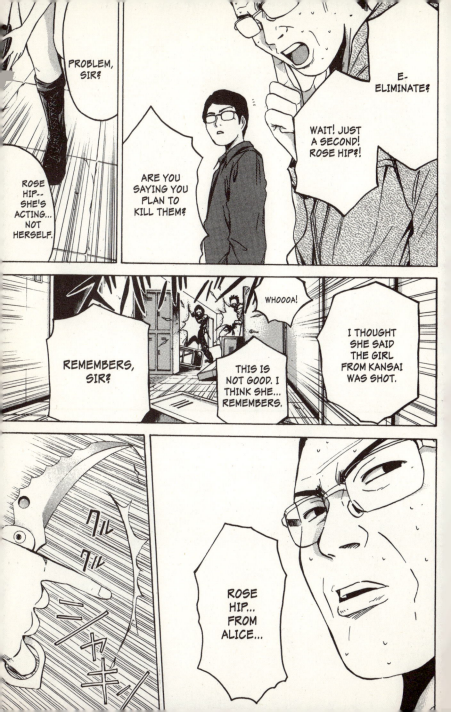

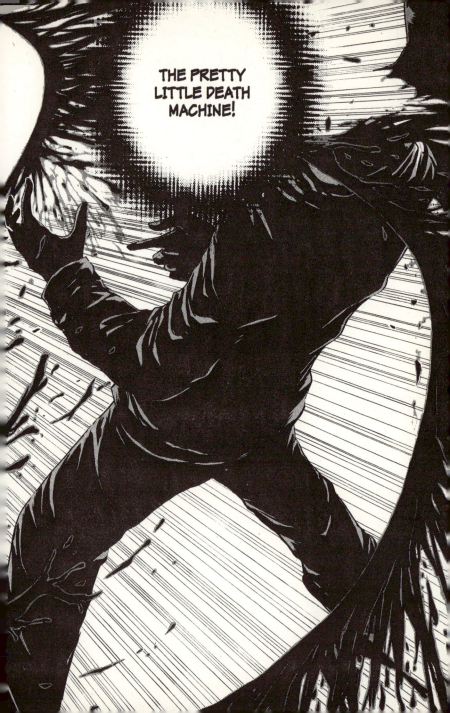

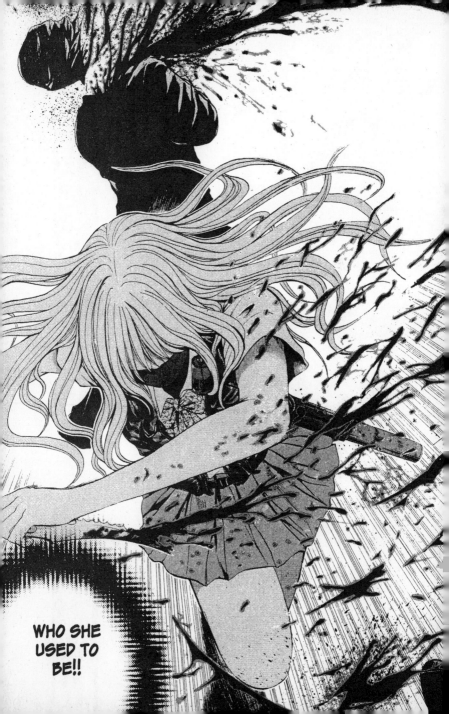

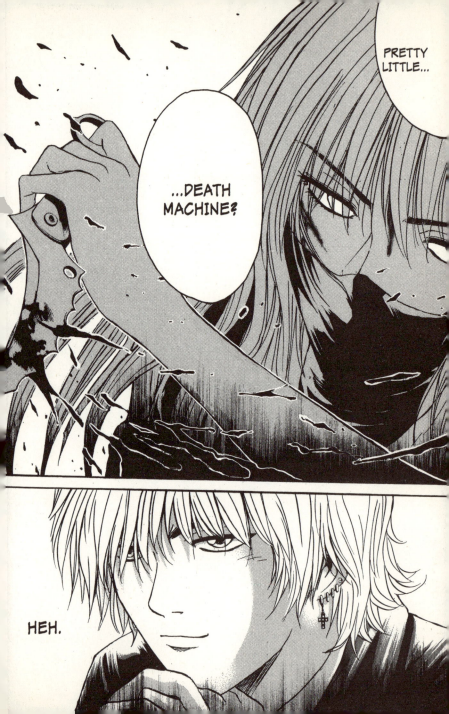

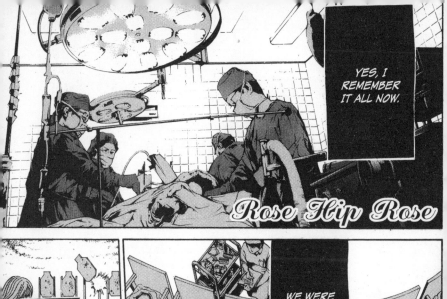

Rose Hip Rose

YES, I REMEMBER IT ALL NOW.

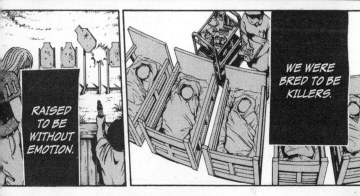

RAISED TO BE WITHOUT EMOTION.

WE WERE BRED TO BE KILLERS.

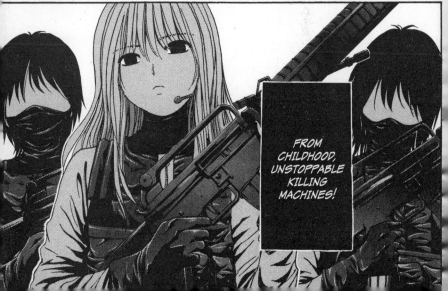

FROM CHILDHOOD, UNSTOPPABLE KILLING MACHINES!

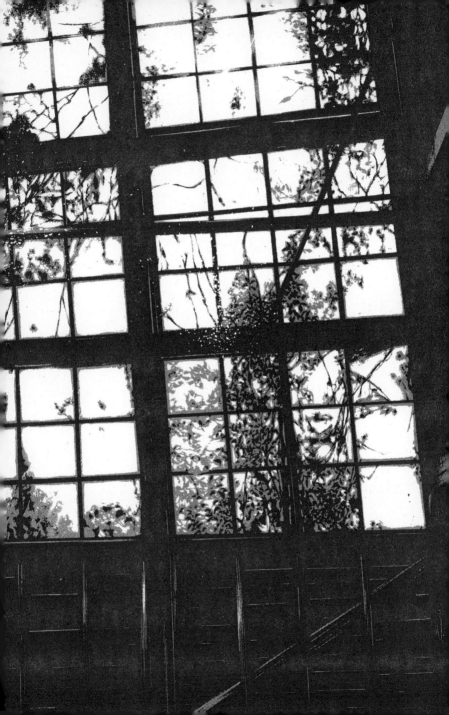

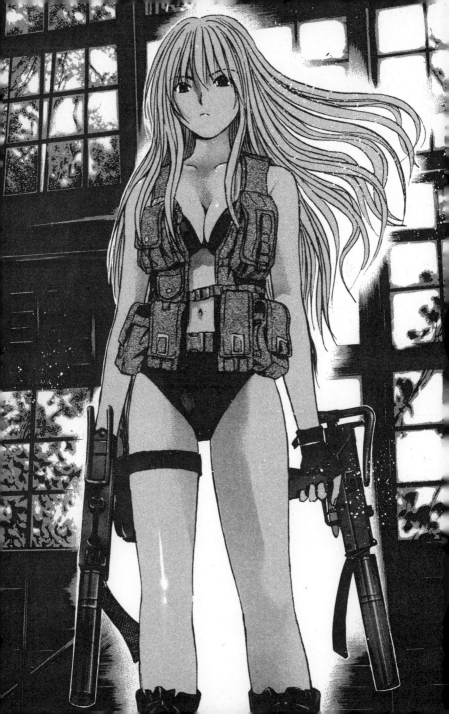

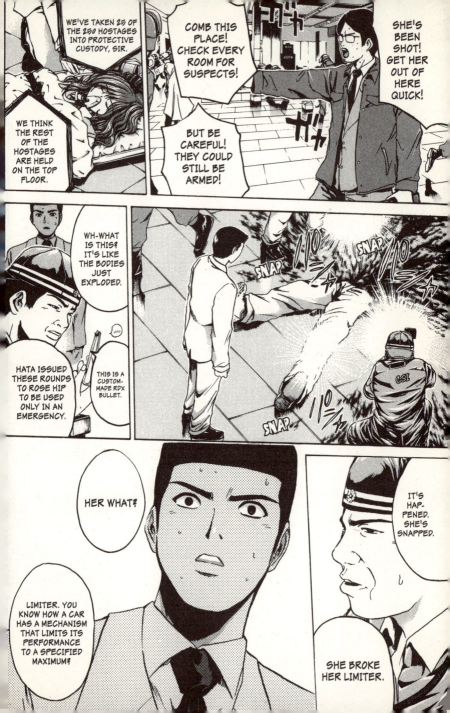

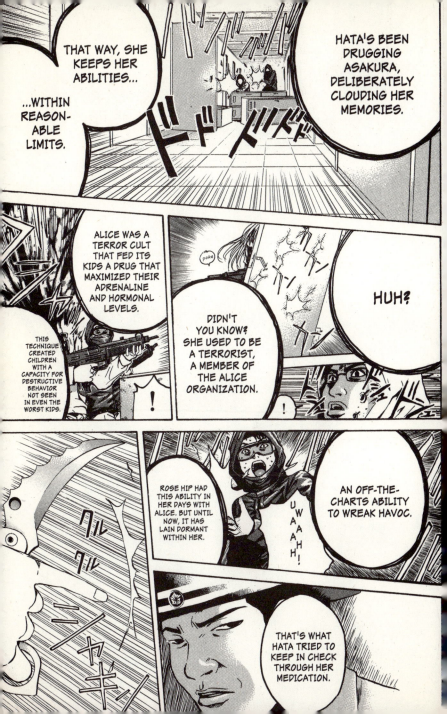

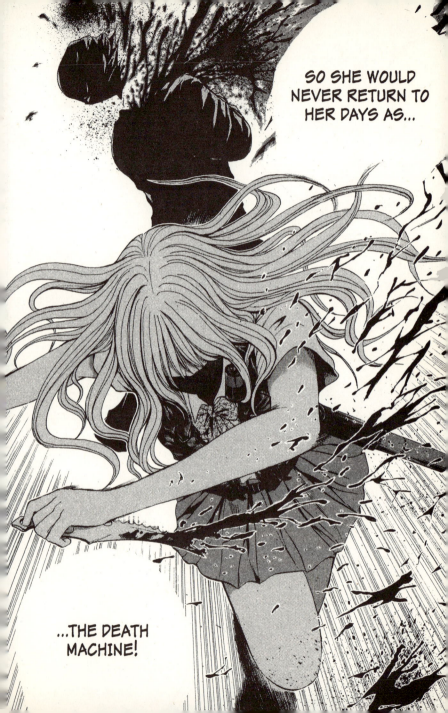

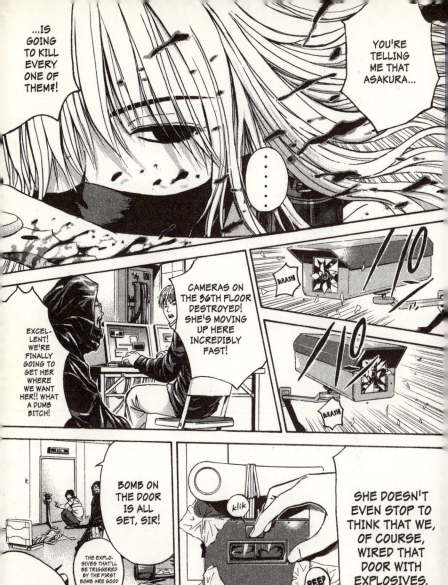

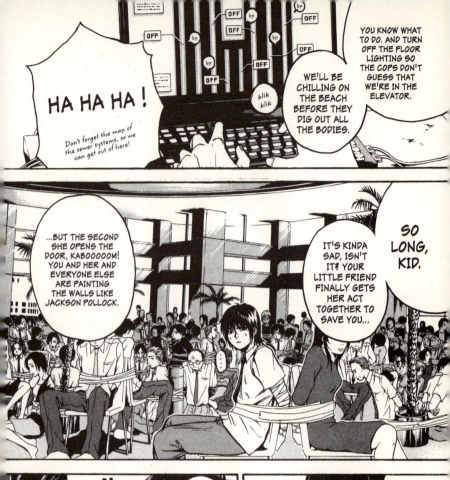

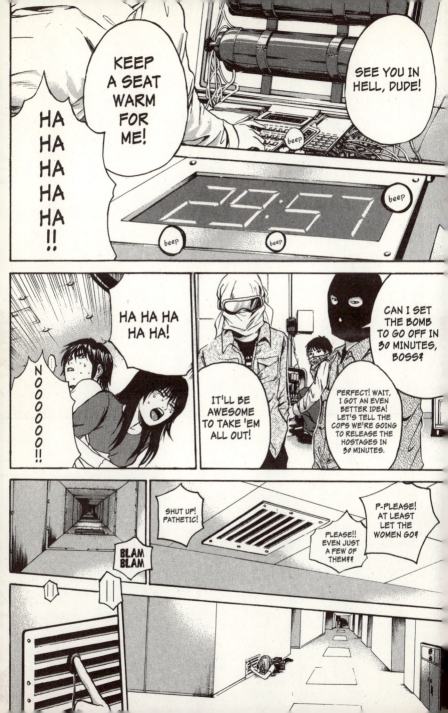

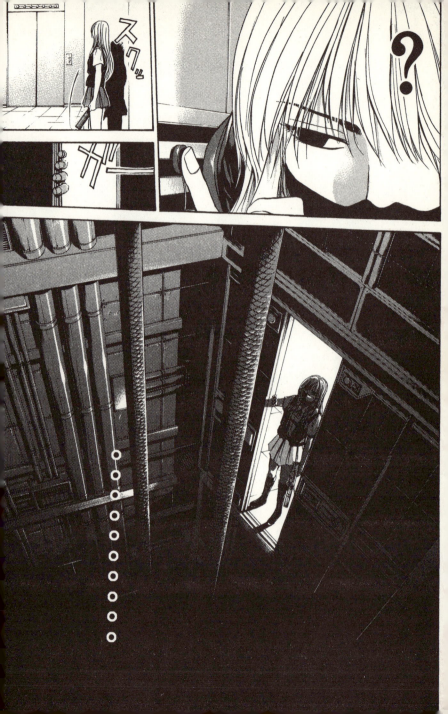

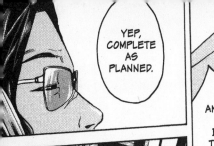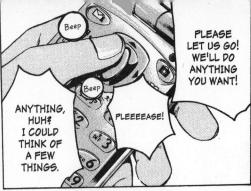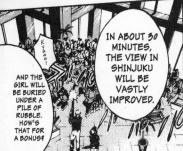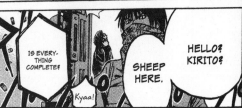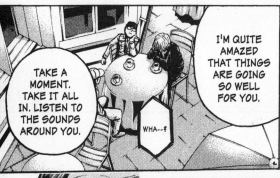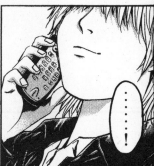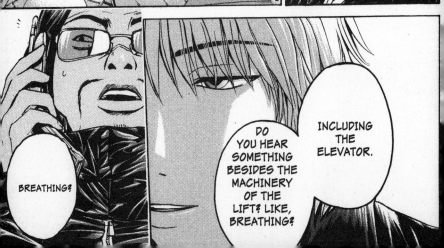

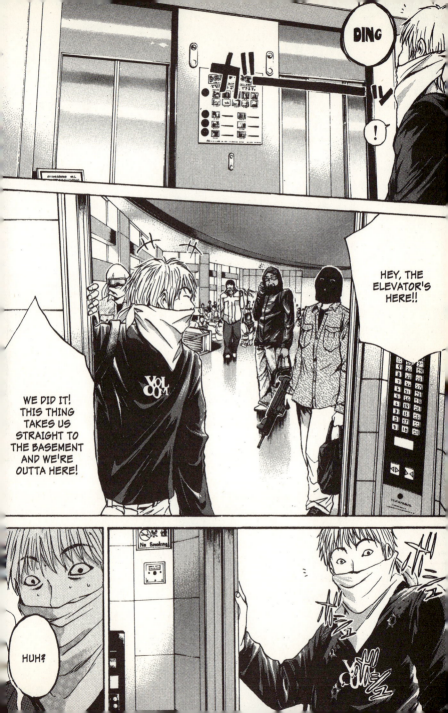

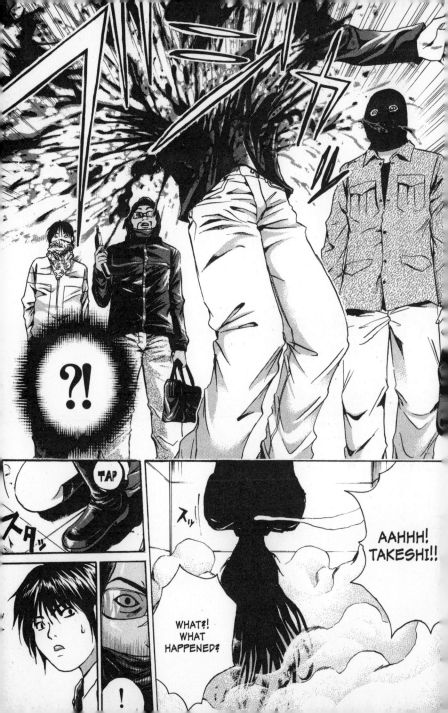

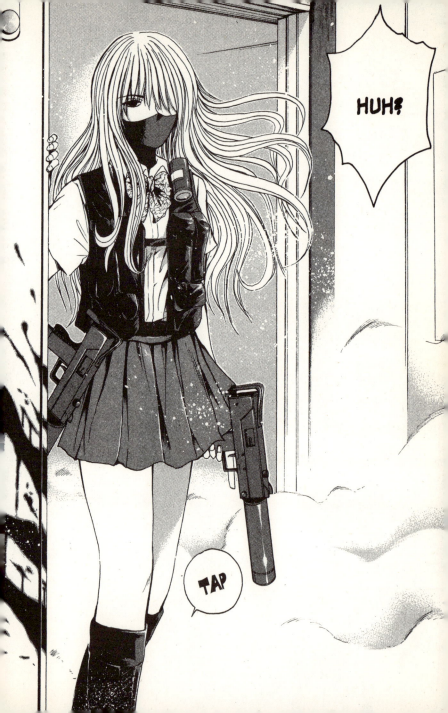

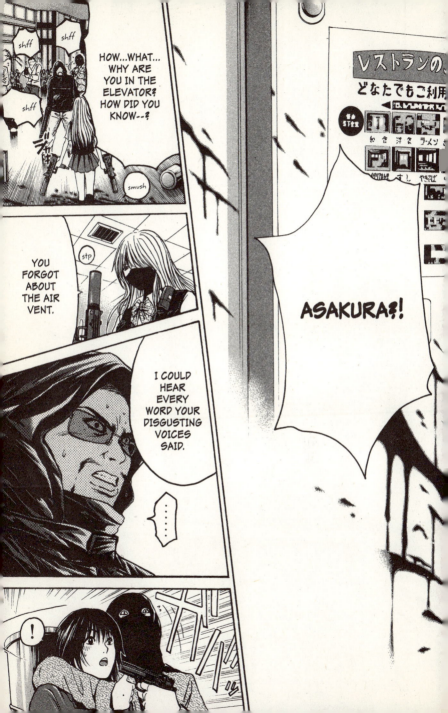

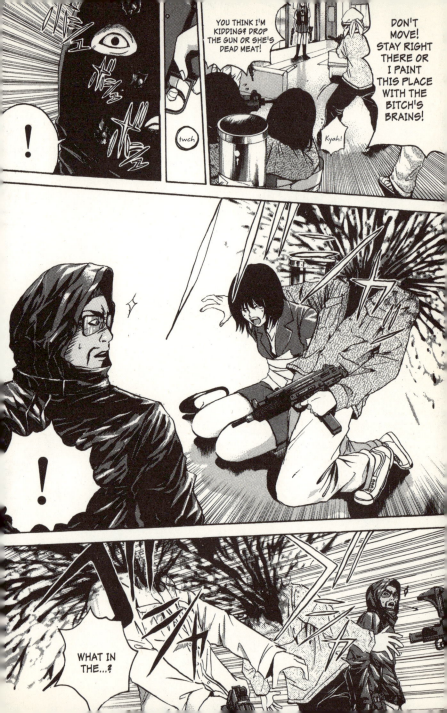

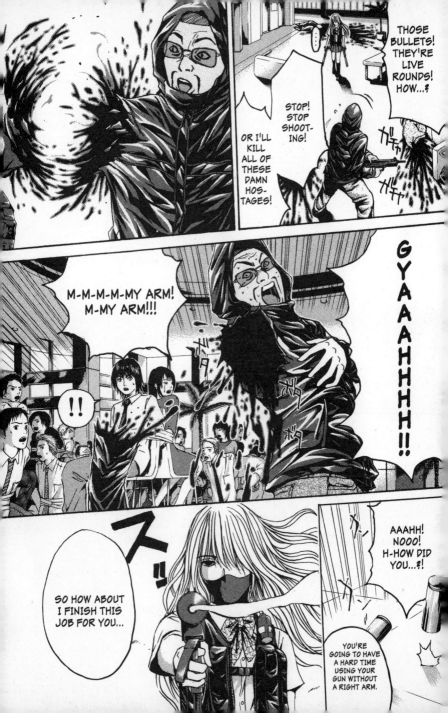

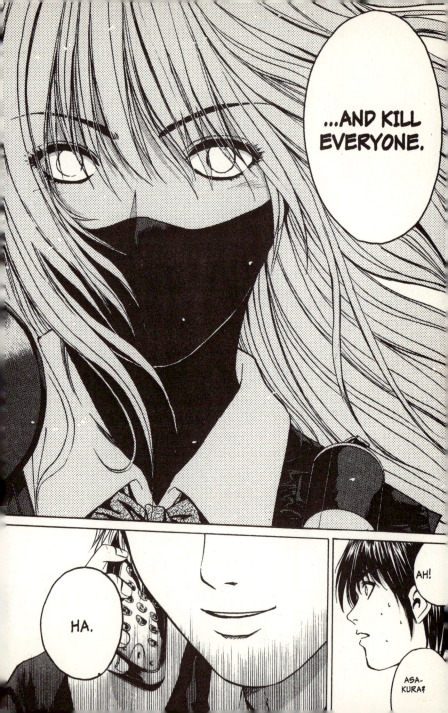

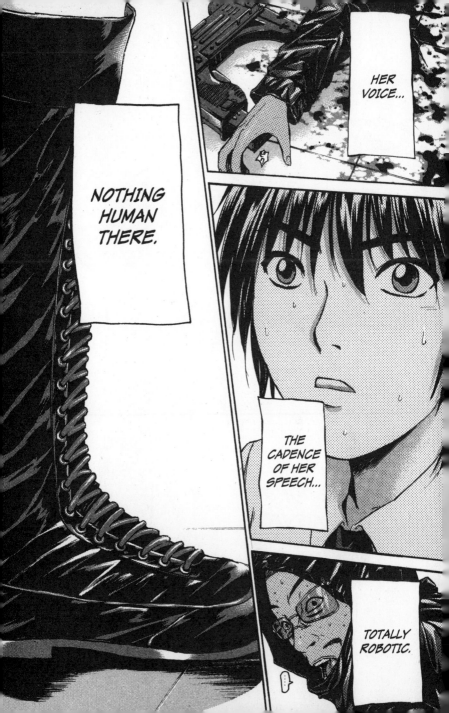

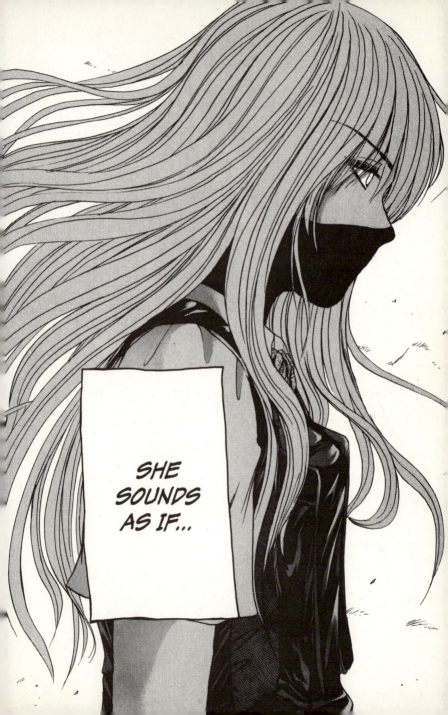

AS IF...

...SHE'S ENJOYING THE
DEATH AND DESTRUCTION!

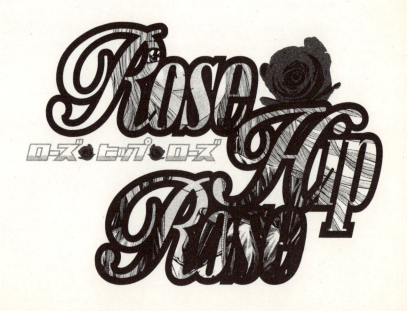

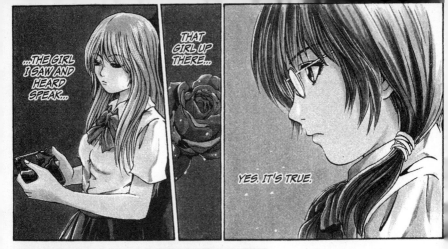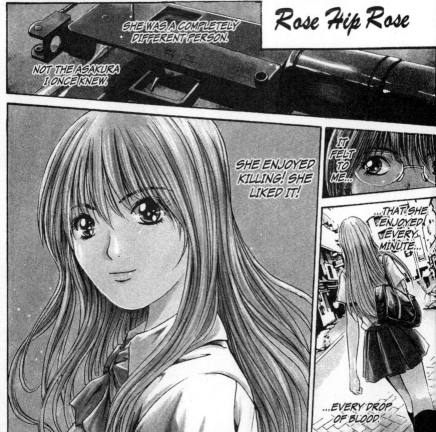

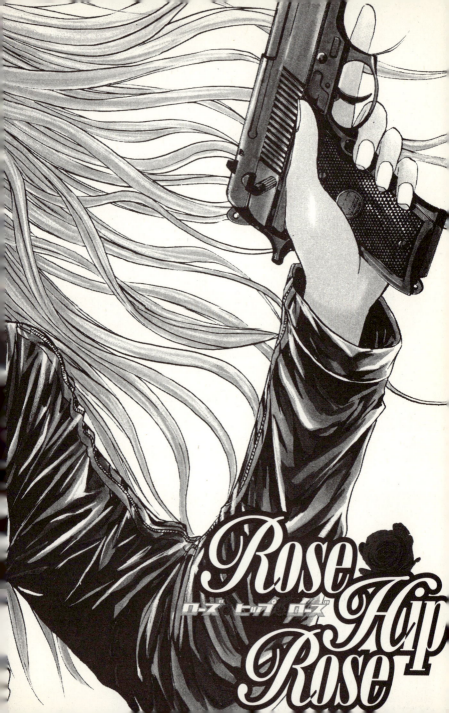

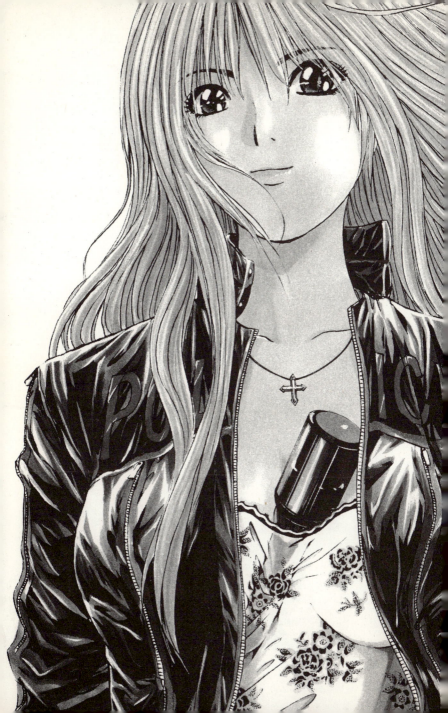

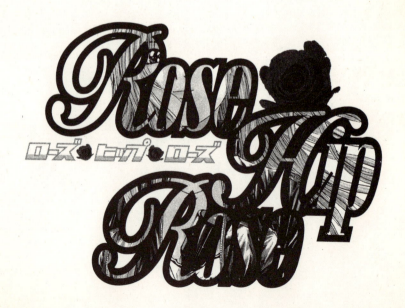

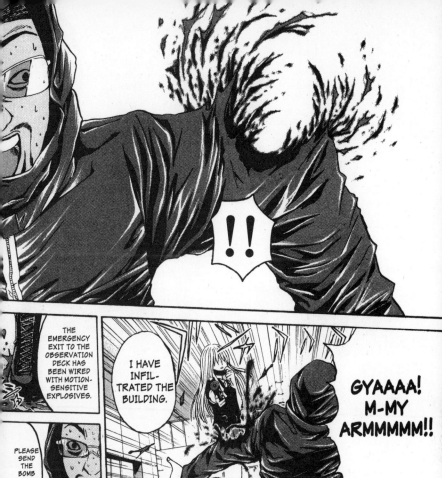

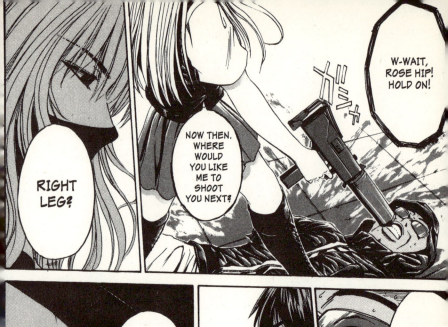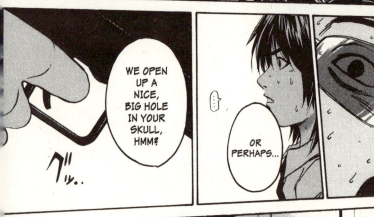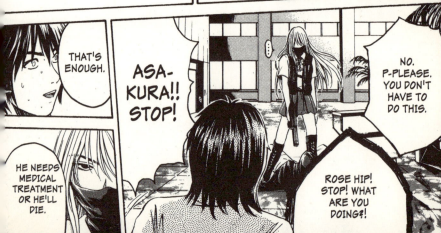

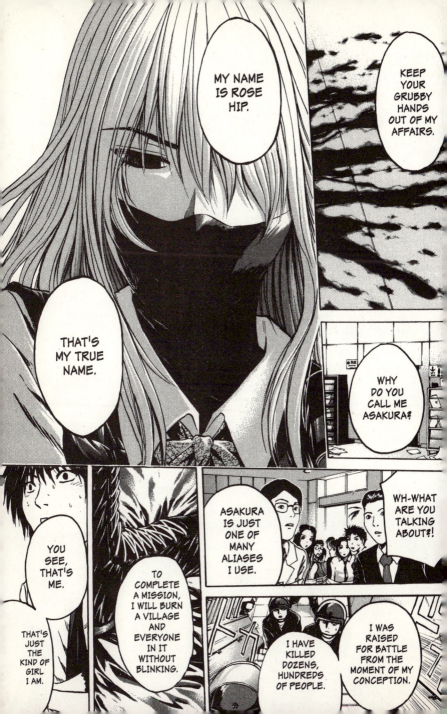

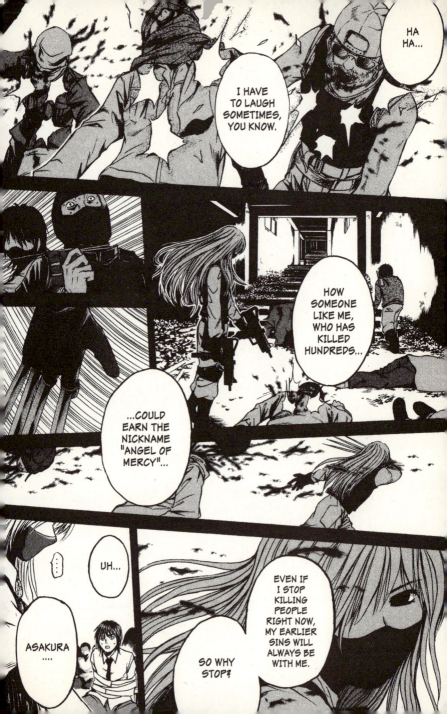

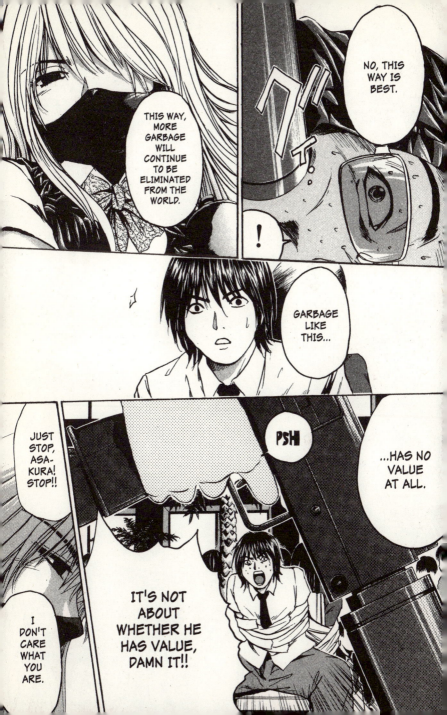

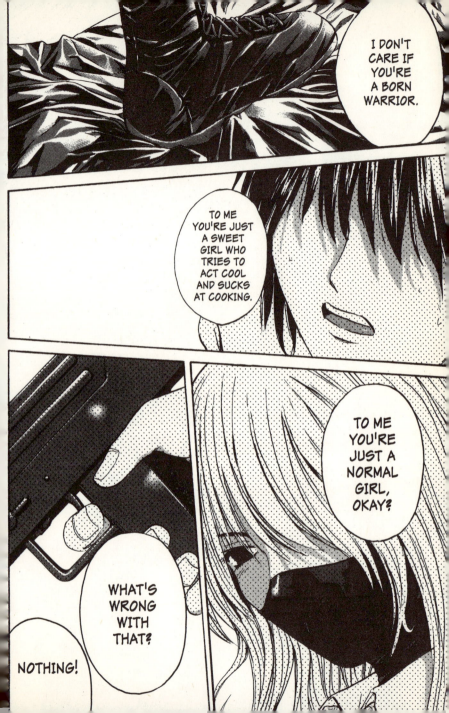

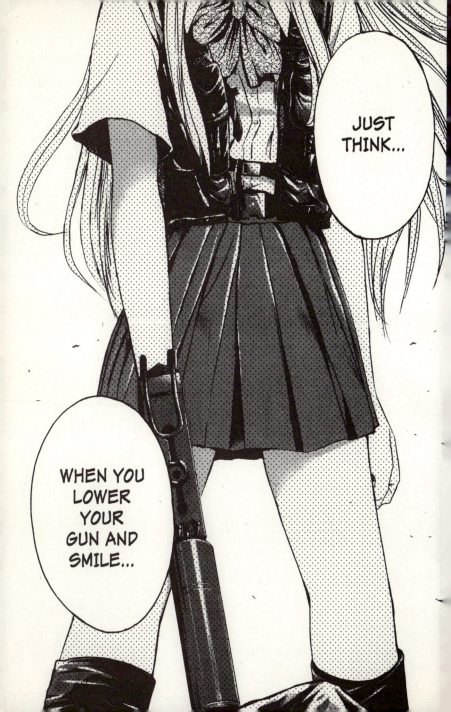

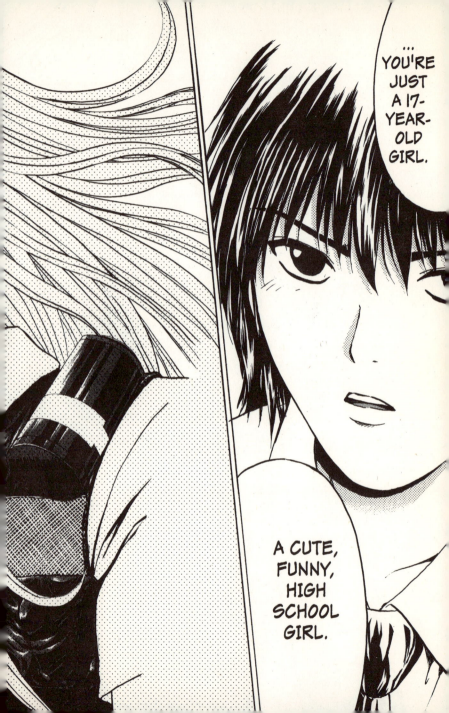

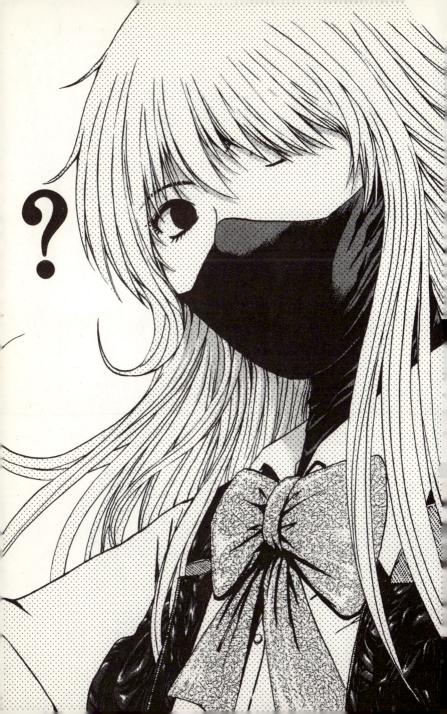

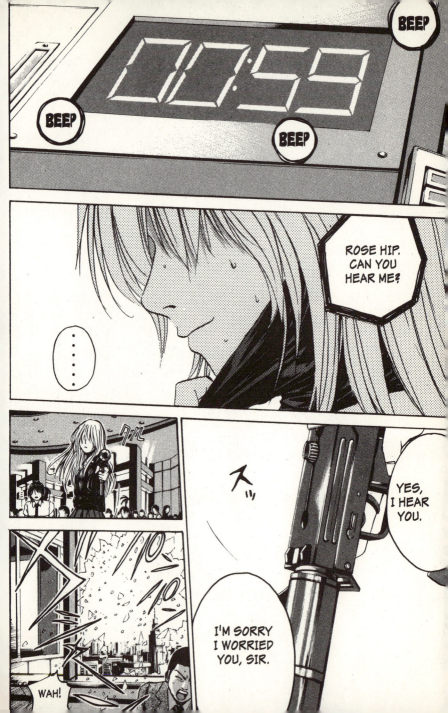

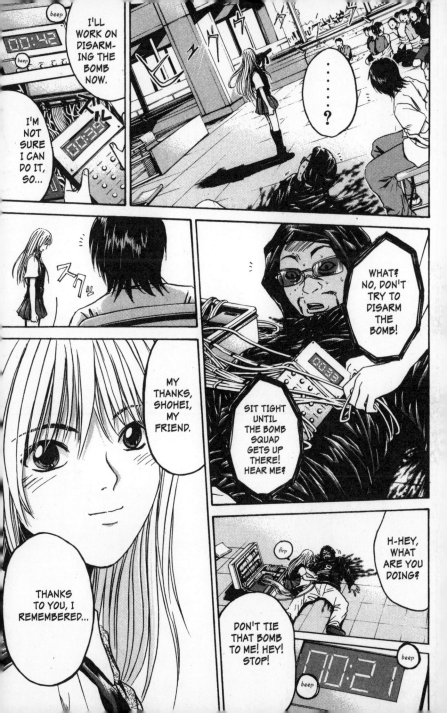

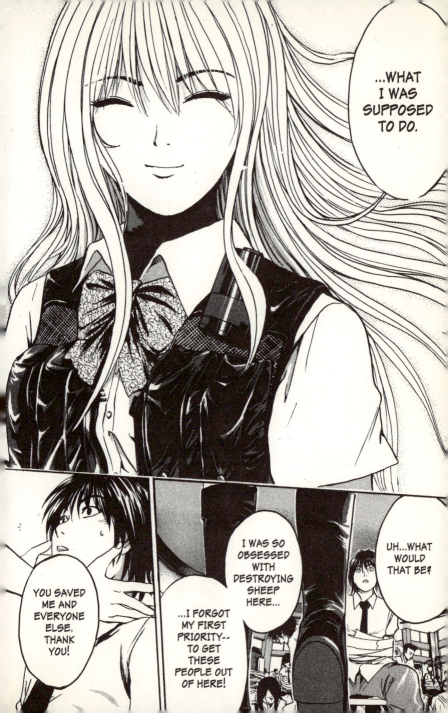

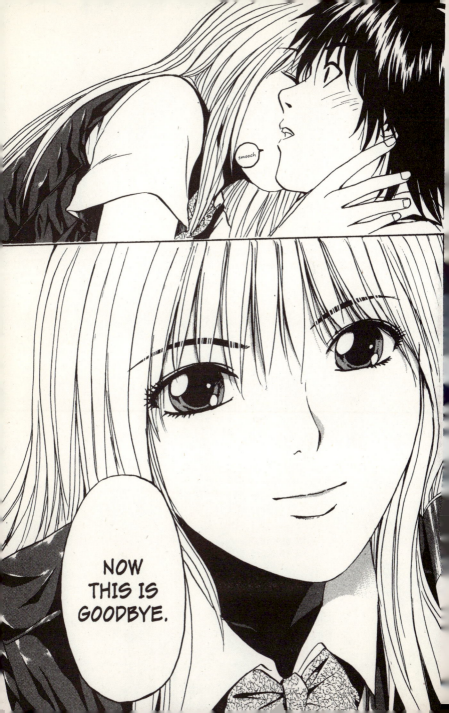

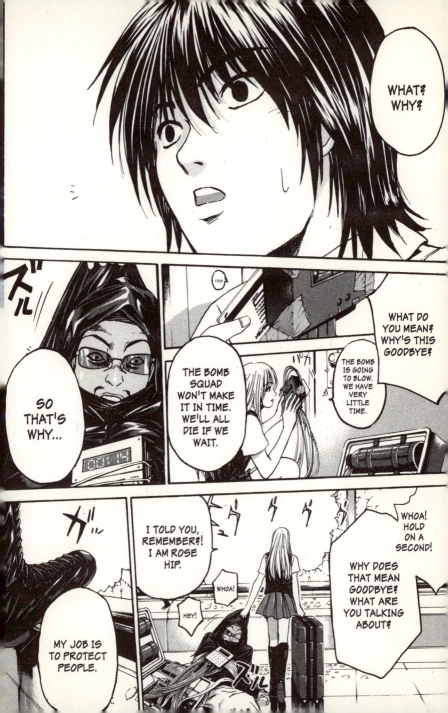

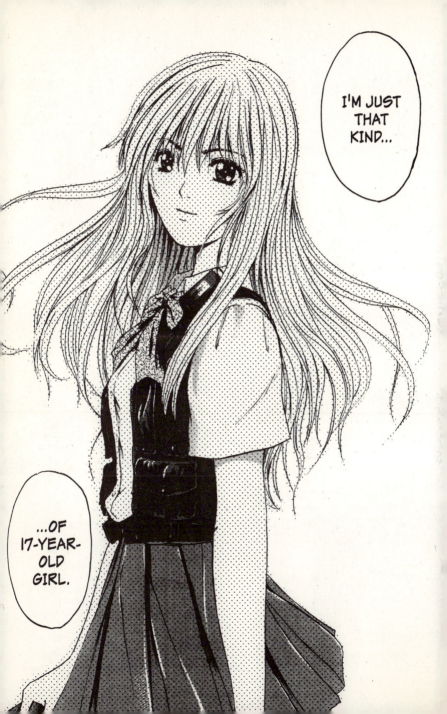

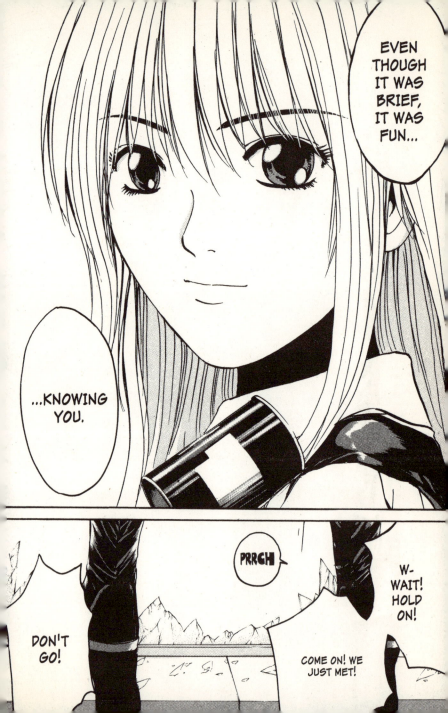

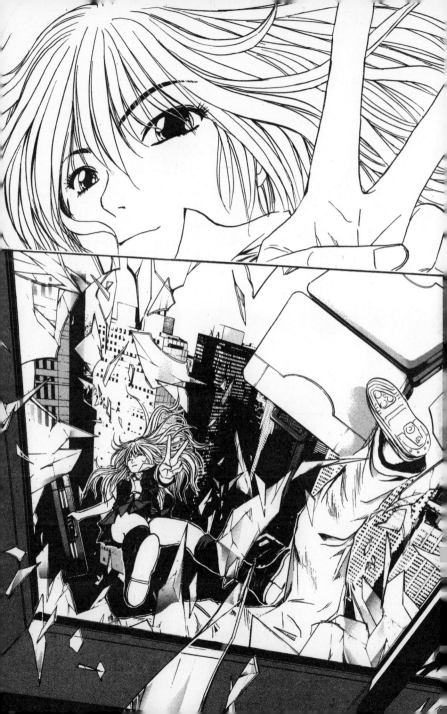

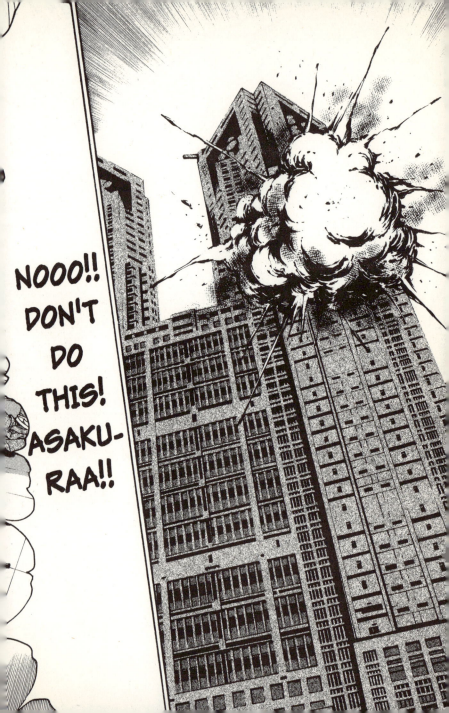

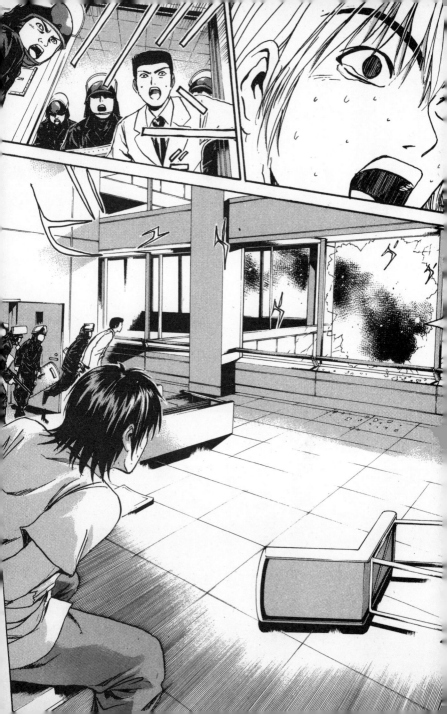

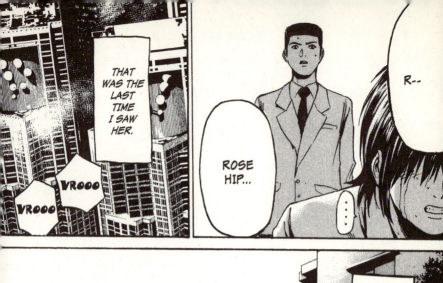
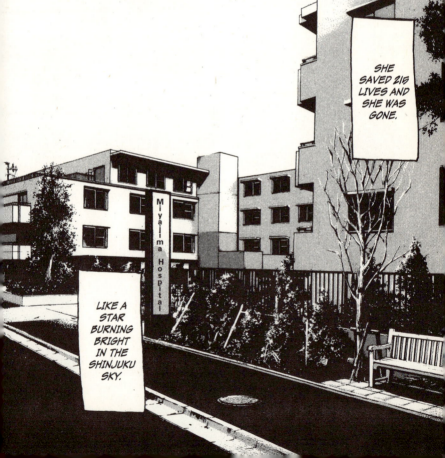

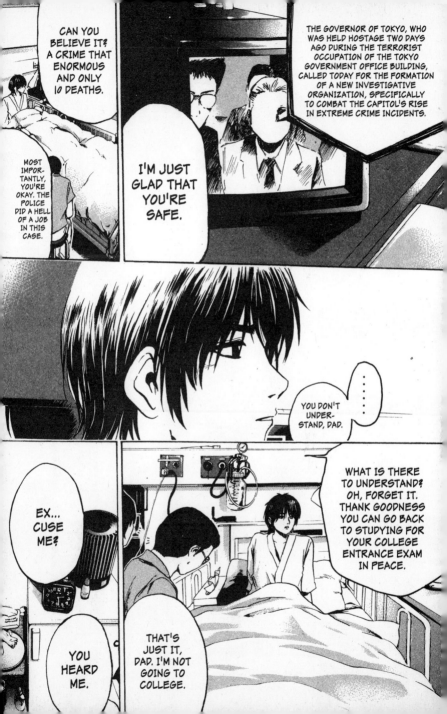

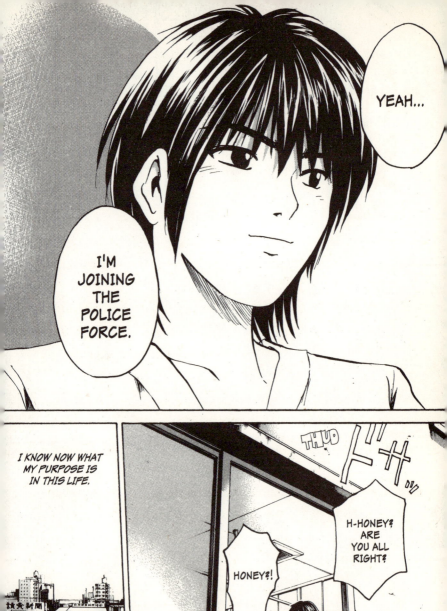

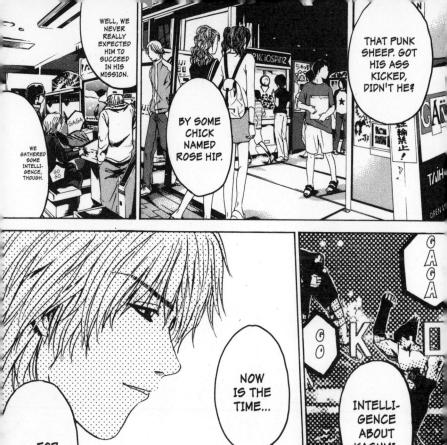

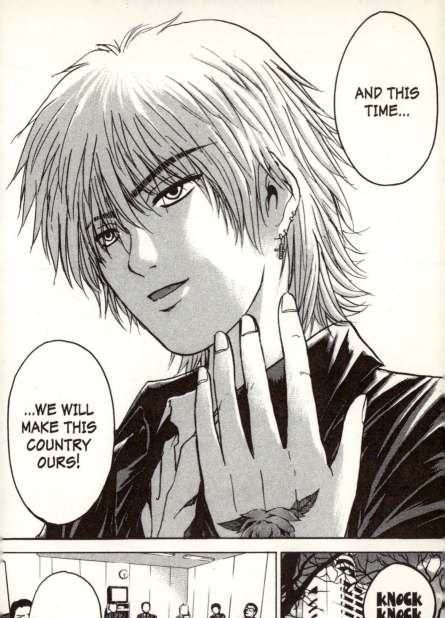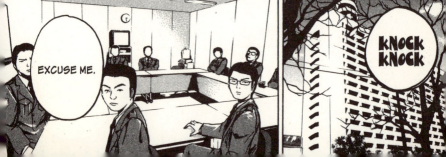

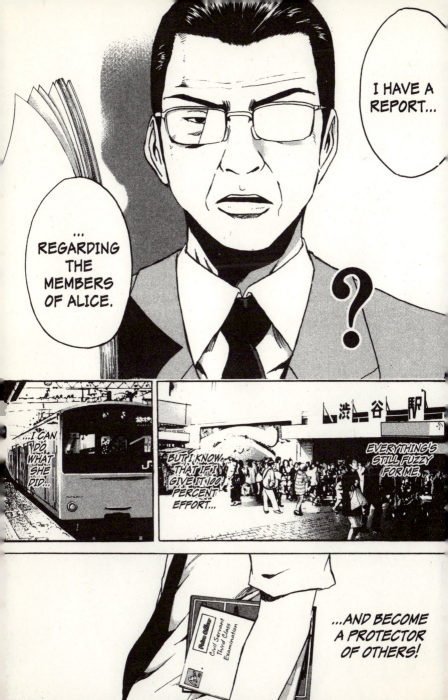

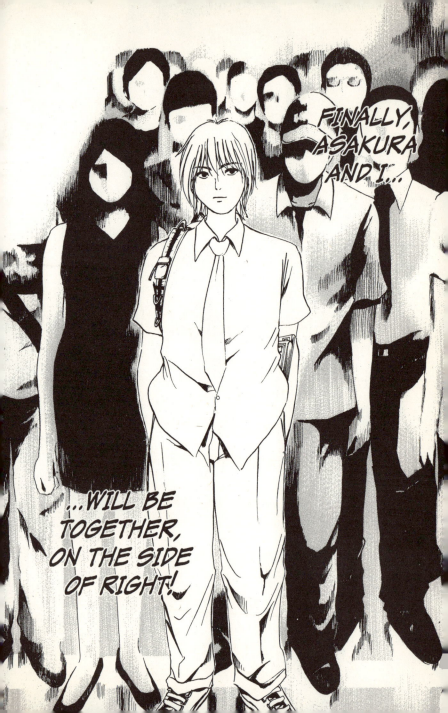

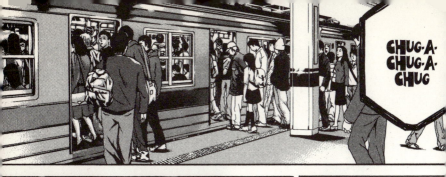

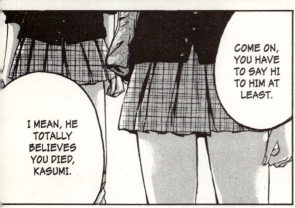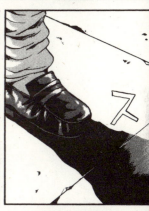

COME ON, YOU HAVE TO SAY HI TO HIM AT LEAST.

I MEAN, HE TOTALLY BELIEVES YOU DIED, KASUMI.

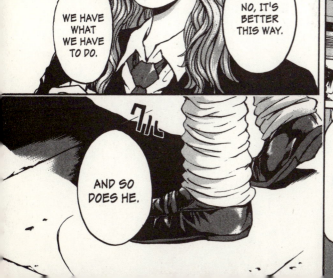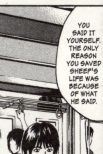

WE HAVE WHAT WE HAVE TO DO.

NO, IT'S BETTER THIS WAY.

YOU SAID IT YOURSELF. THE ONLY REASON YOU SAVED SHEEP'S LIFE WAS BECAUSE OF WHAT HE SAID.

AND SO DOES HE.

SO YOU GOTTA AT LEAST TELL HIM WHERE YOU ARE.

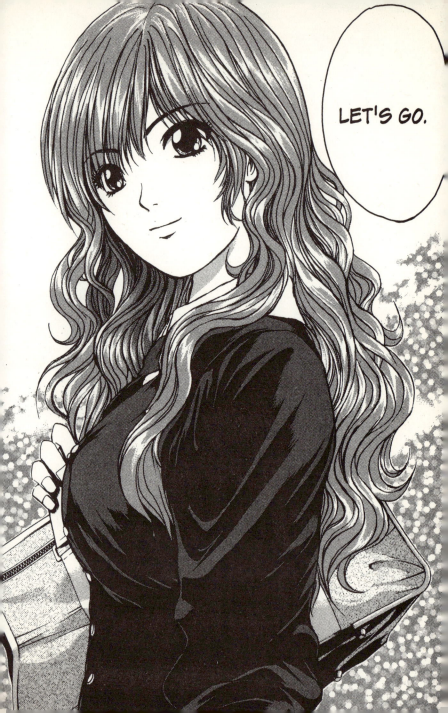

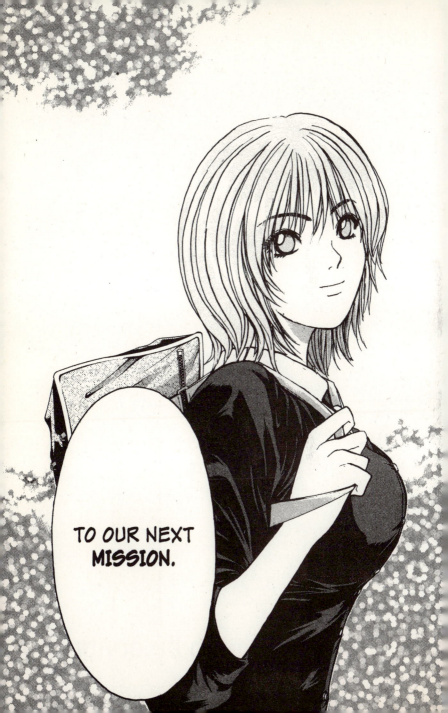

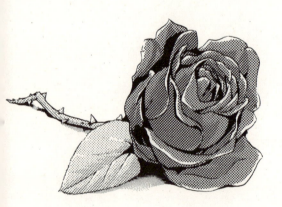

....To be continued

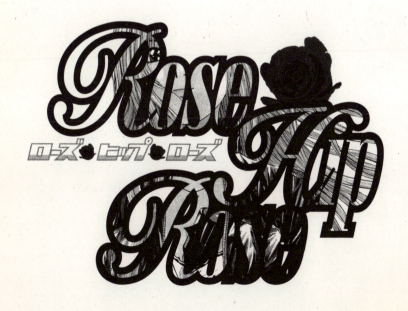

SPECIAL AUTHOR'S NOTE:

ROSE HIP ROSE BEGAN ITS RUN IN *YOUNG MAGAZINE UPPERS* IN NOVEMBER OF 2002. BUT WHEN THAT MAGAZINE STOPPED PUBLISHING, THE STORY OF *ROSE HIP ROSE* CAME TO A PREMATURE BUT UNAVOIDABLE END.
WHAT YOU ARE ABOUT TO READ IS THE NEXT CHAPTER IN THE *ROSE HIP ROSE* ADVENTURE. THIS SERIES, TITLED *MAGNUM ROSE HIP*, WAS PICKED UP BY *WEEKLY SHONEN MAGAZINE*. BUT IT HAS NEVER BEEN COLLECTED IN GRAPHIC NOVEL FORM. UNTIL NOW.
ENJOY!

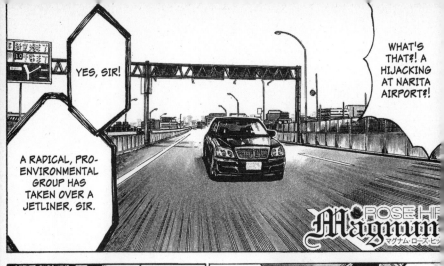

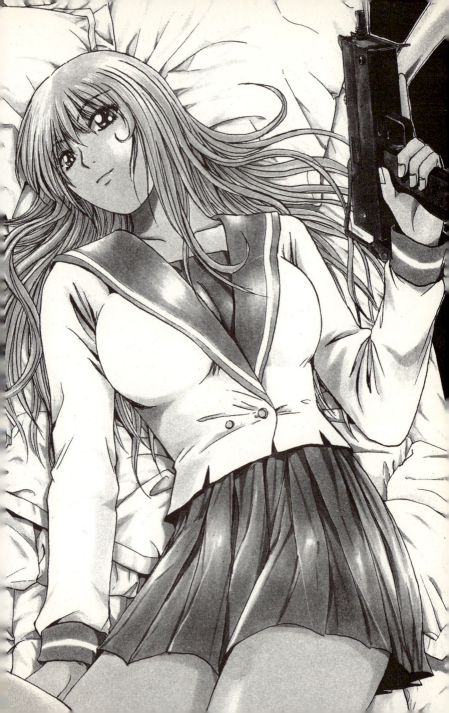

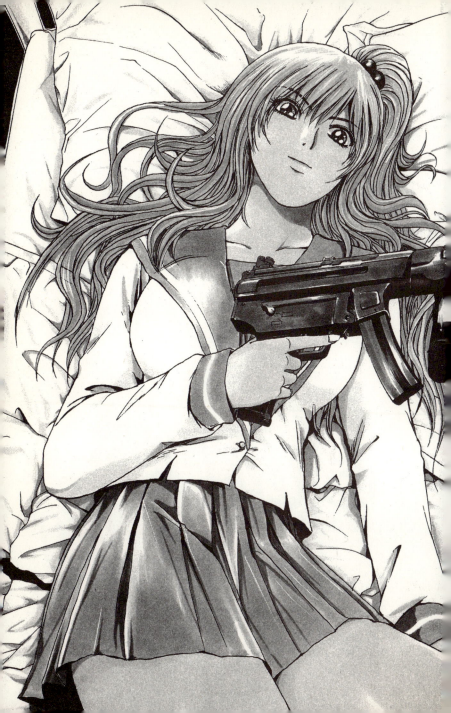

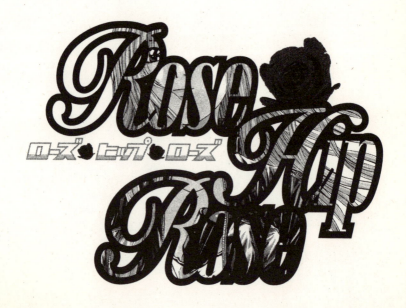

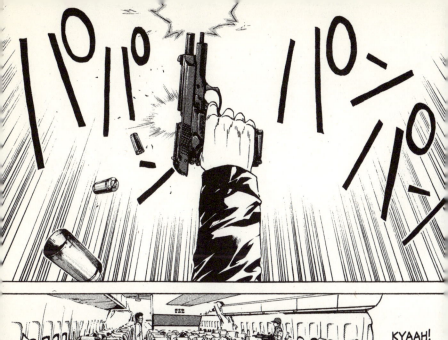

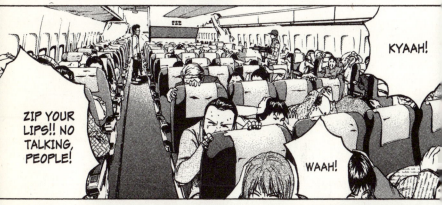

KYAAH!

ZIP YOUR LIPS!! NO TALKING, PEOPLE!

WAAH!

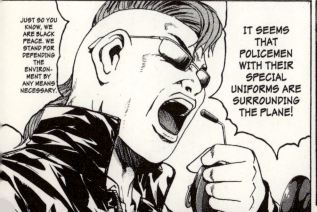

JUST SO YOU KNOW, WE ARE BLACK PEACE. WE STAND FOR DEFENDING THE ENVIRONMENT BY ANY MEANS NECESSARY.

IT SEEMS THAT POLICEMEN WITH THEIR SPECIAL UNIFORMS ARE SURROUNDING THE PLANE!

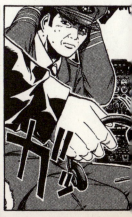

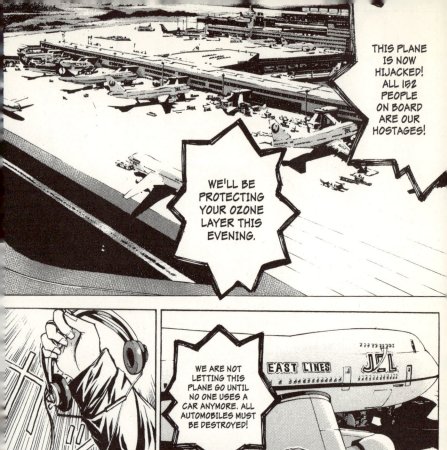
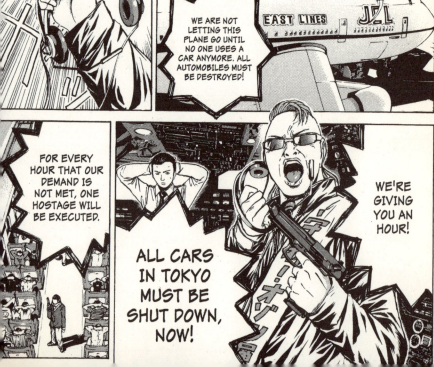

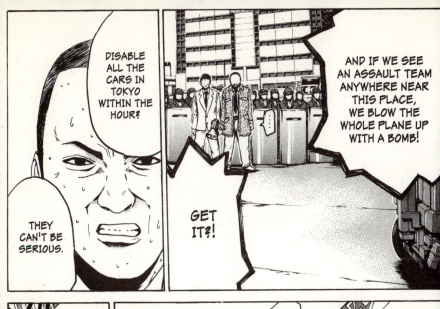
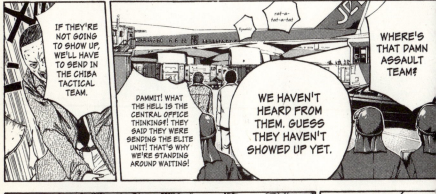
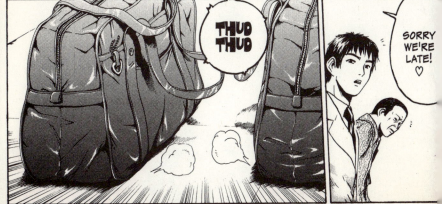

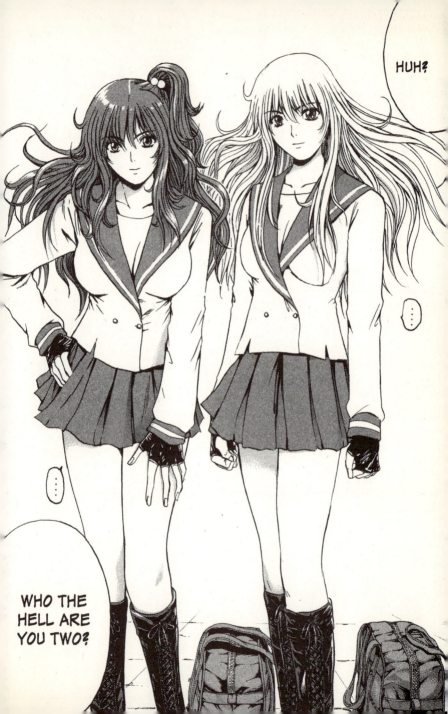

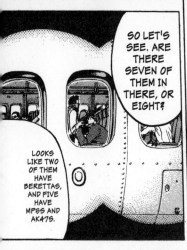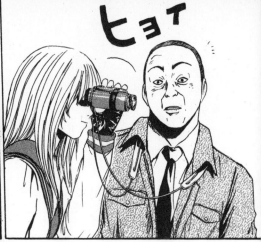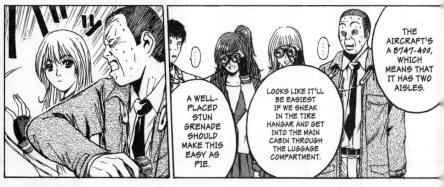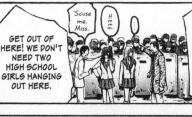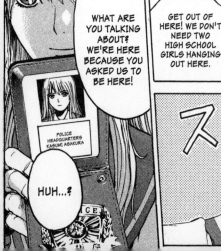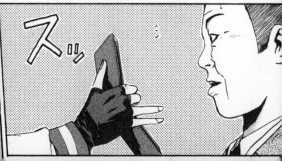

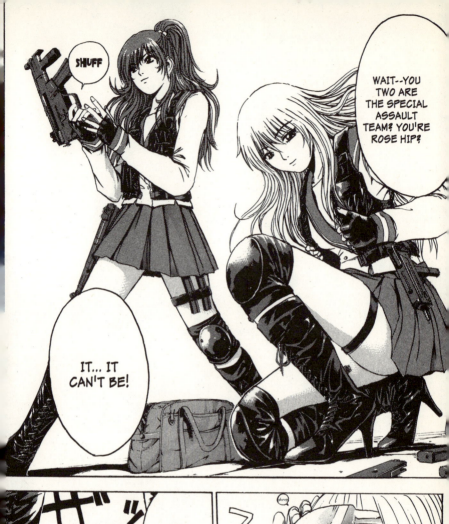
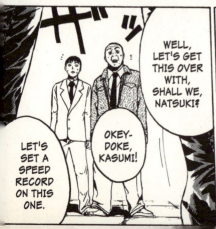
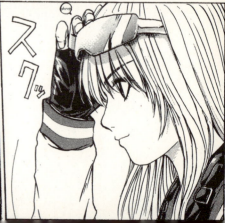

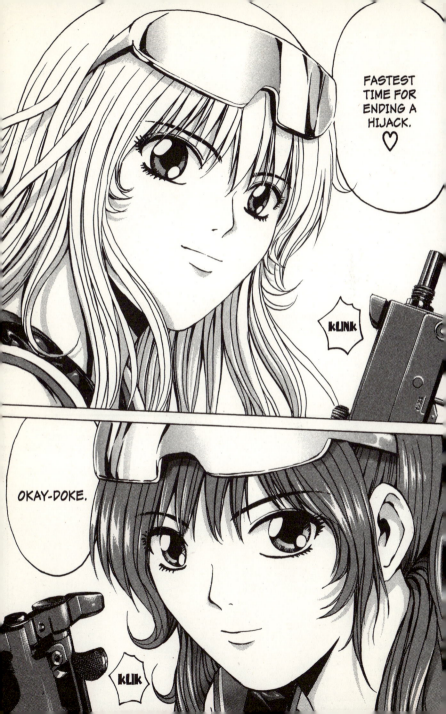

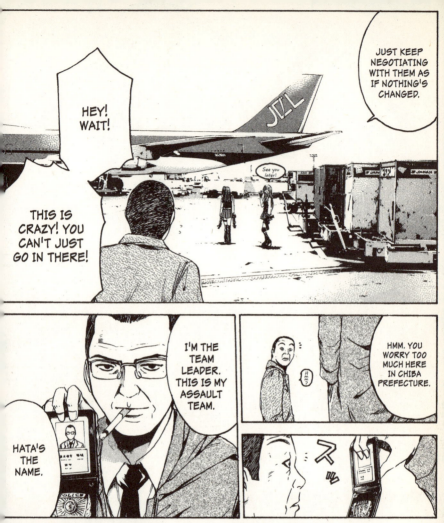
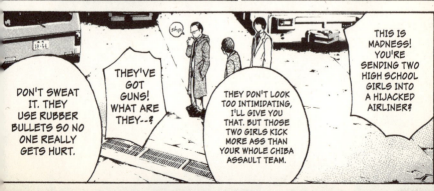

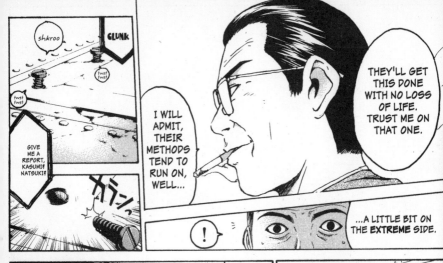

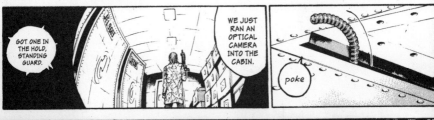

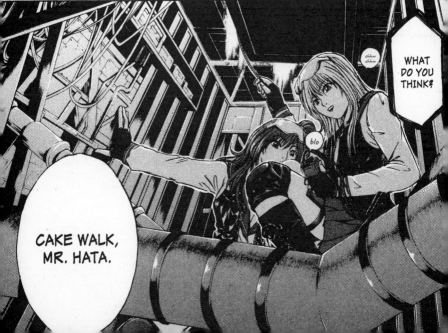

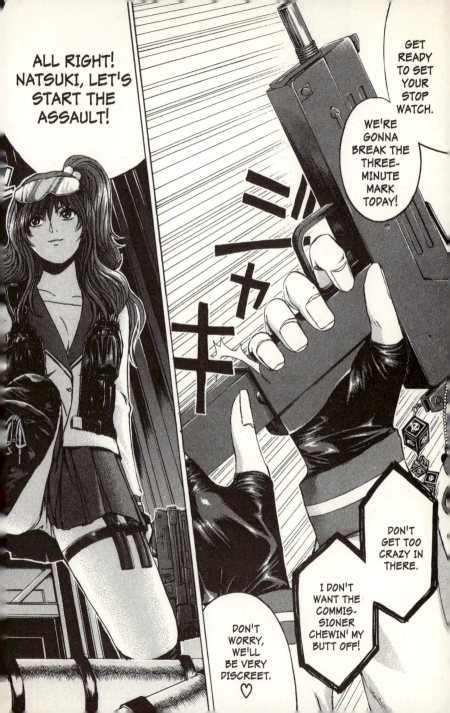

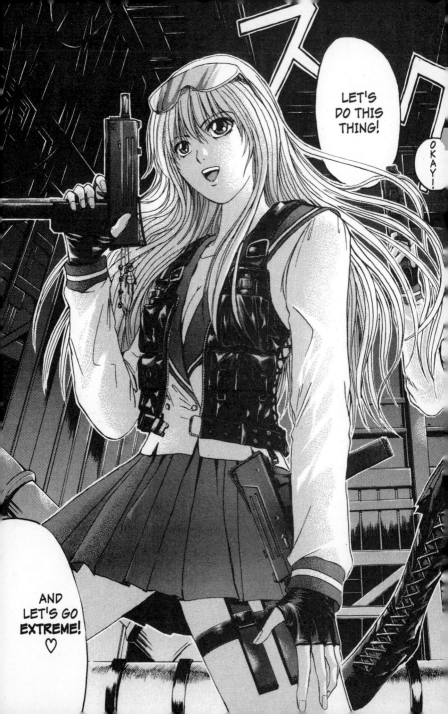

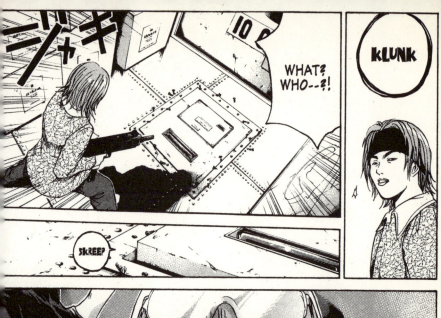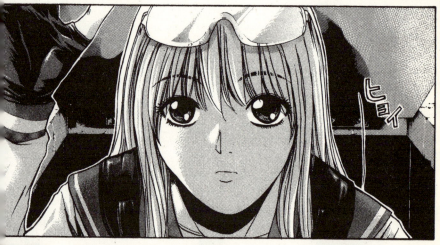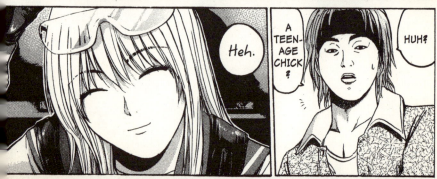

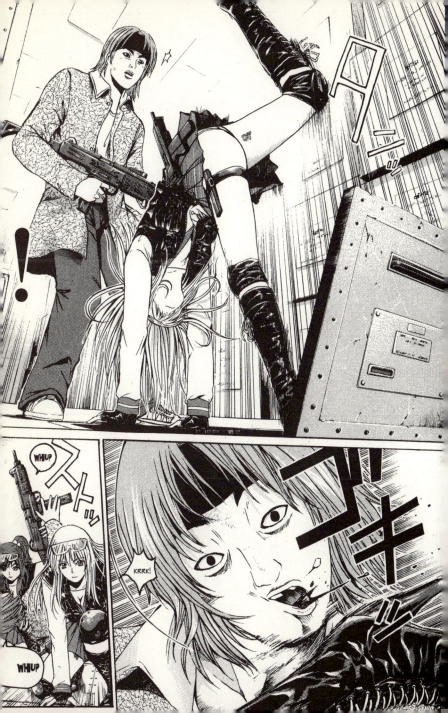

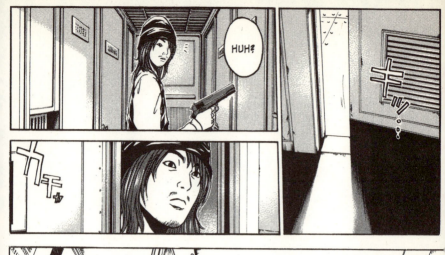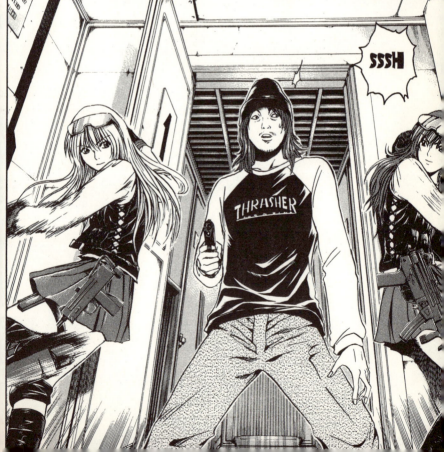

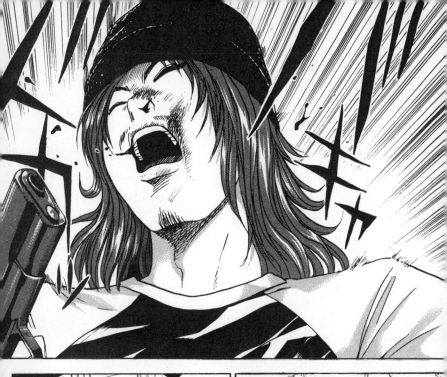

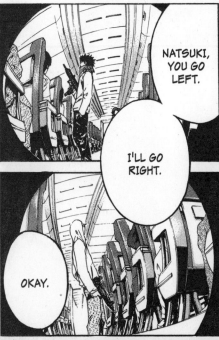

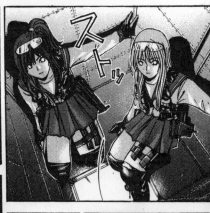

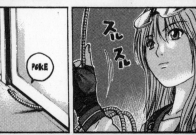

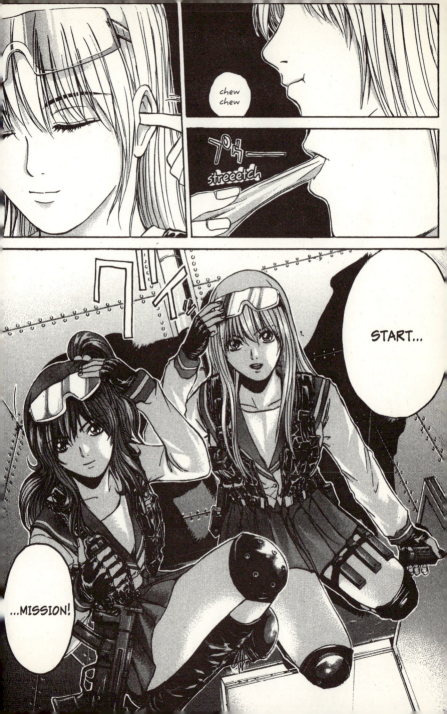

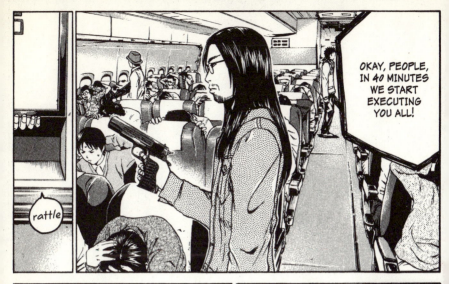
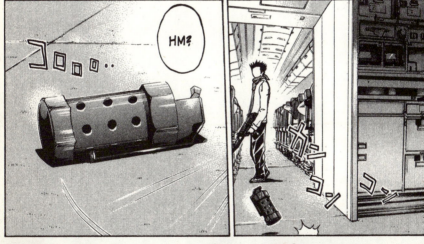
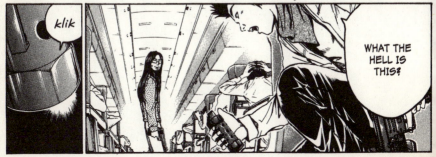

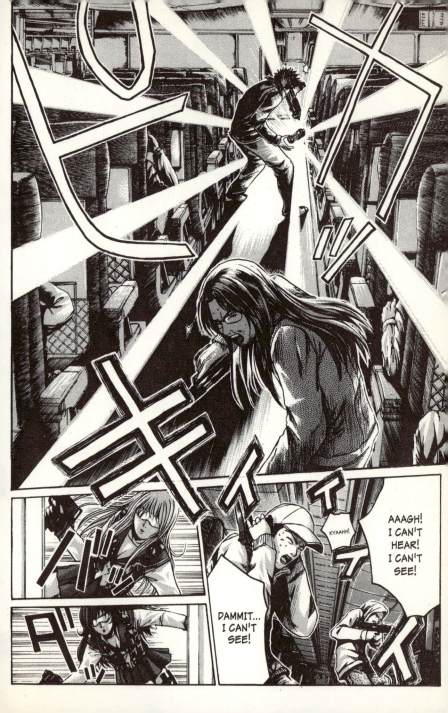

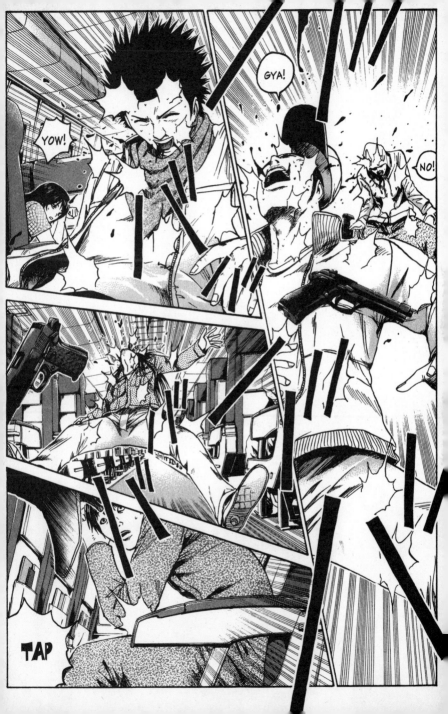

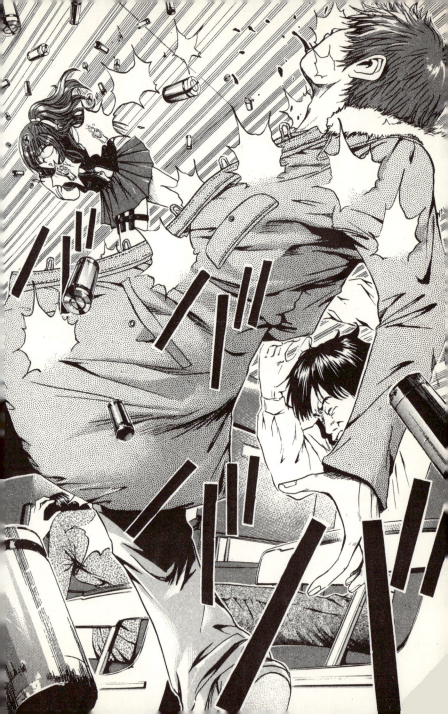

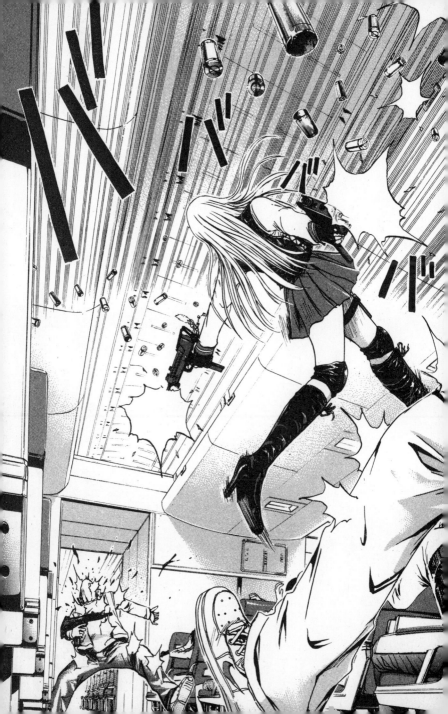

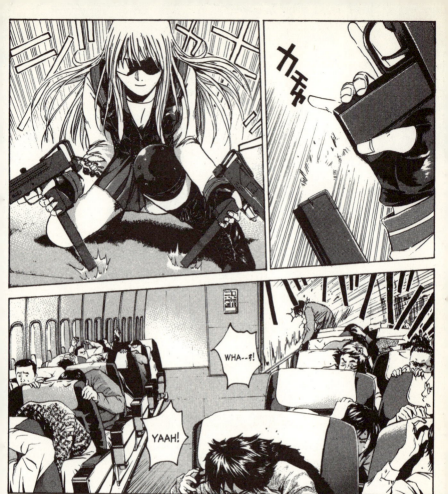
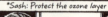
*Sash: Protect the ozone layer
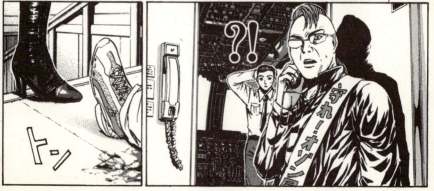

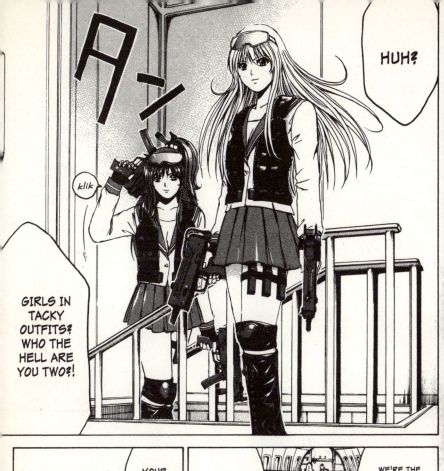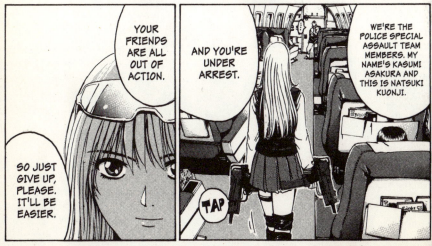

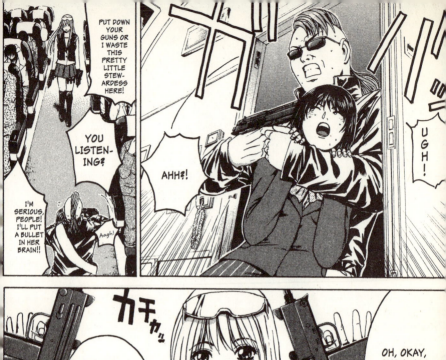
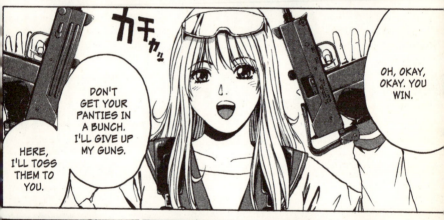
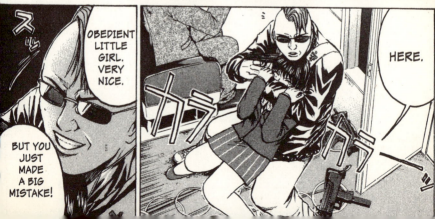

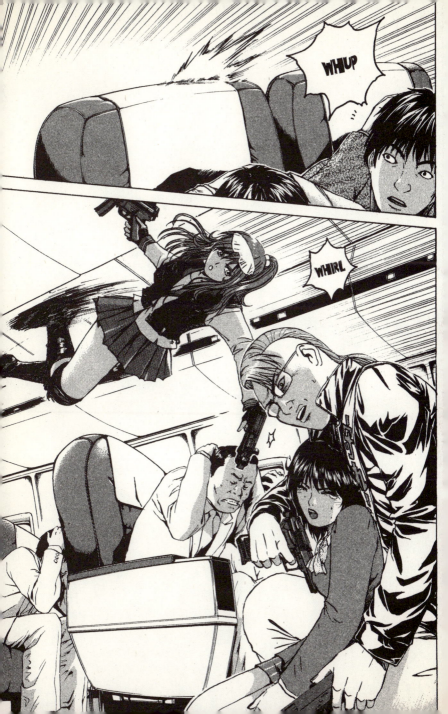

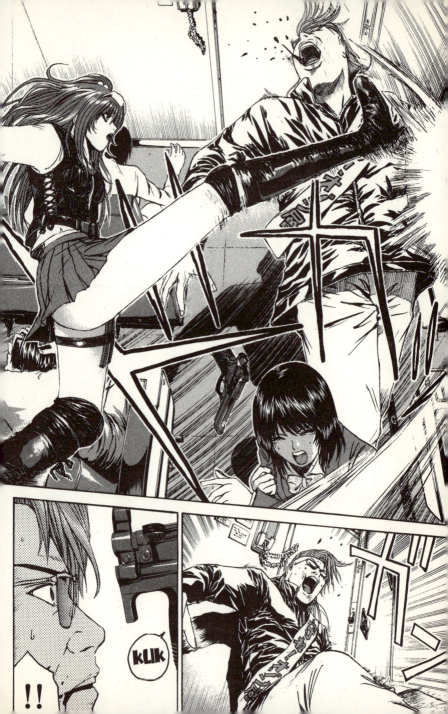

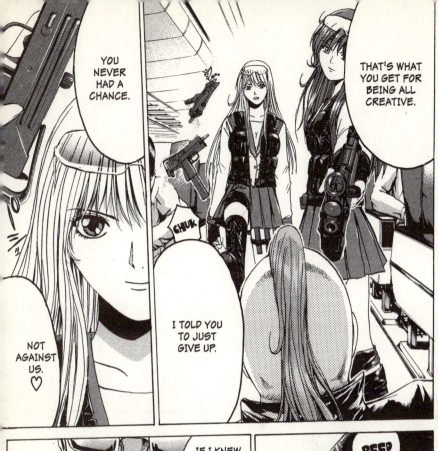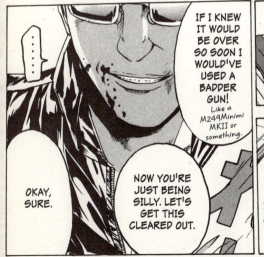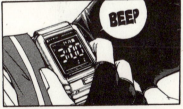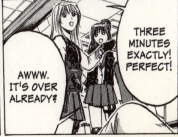

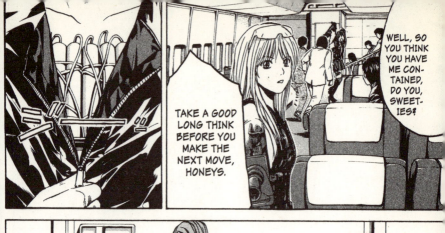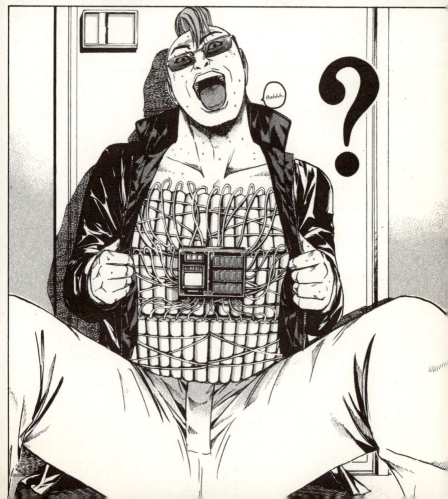

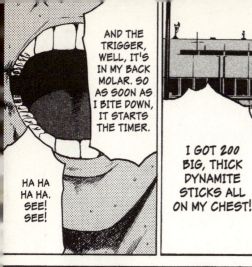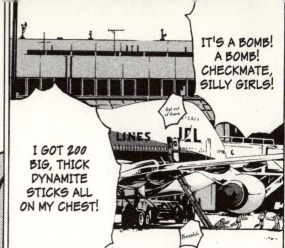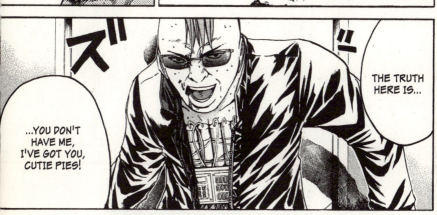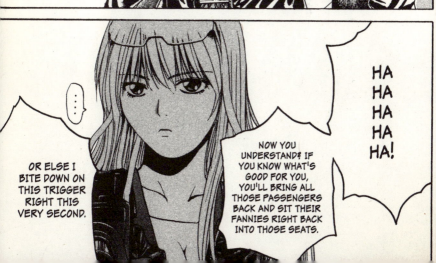

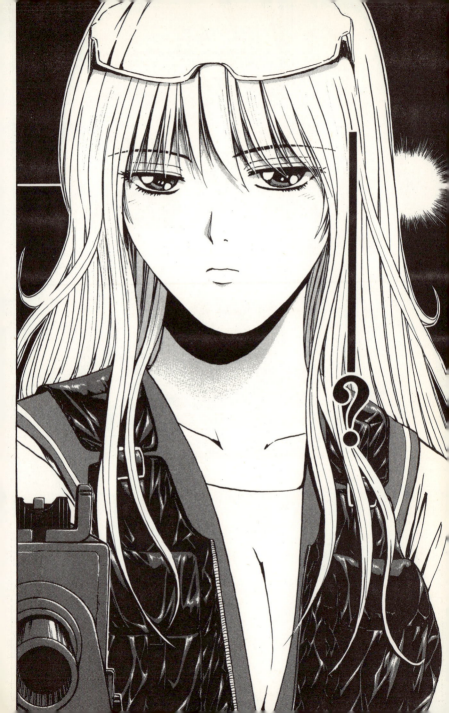

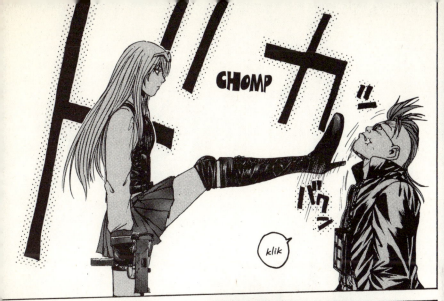
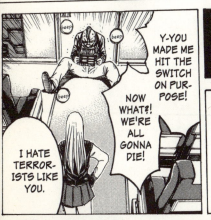
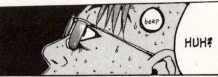
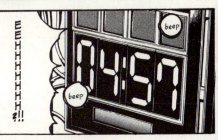
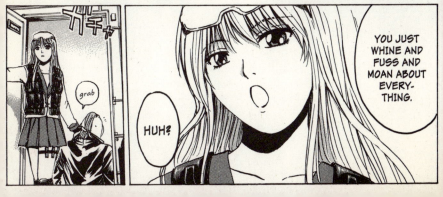

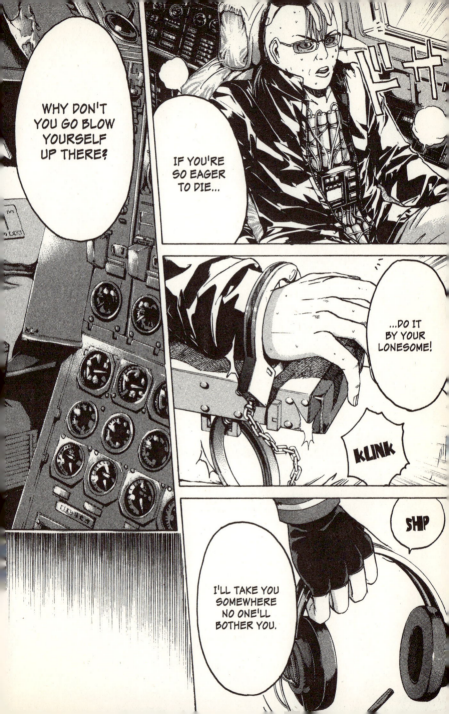

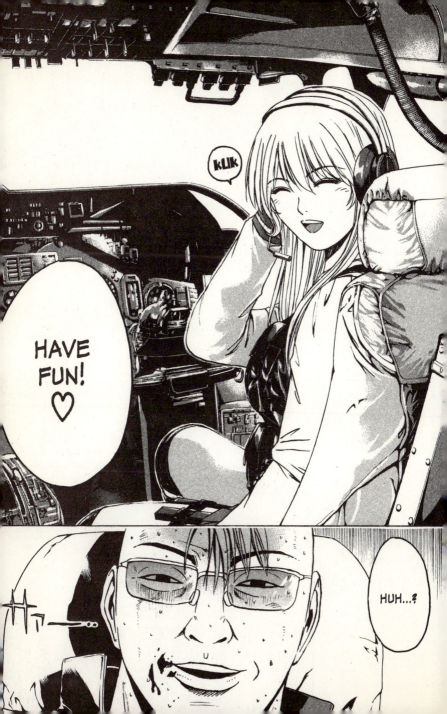

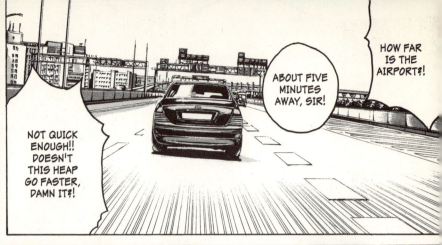

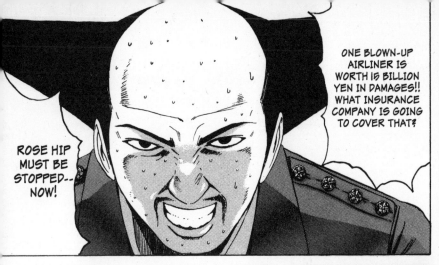
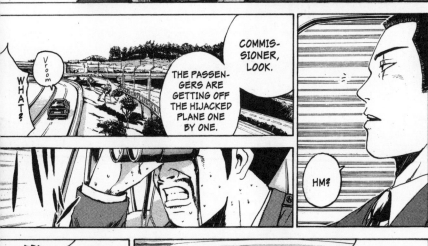
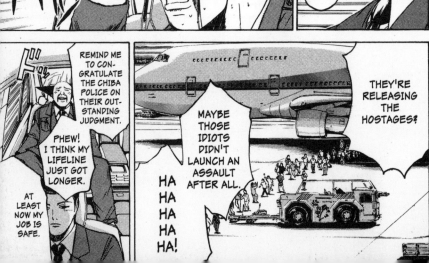

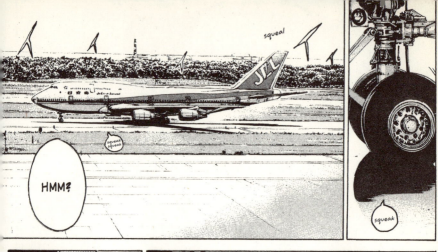
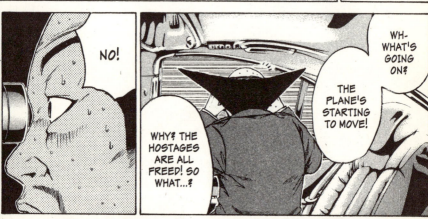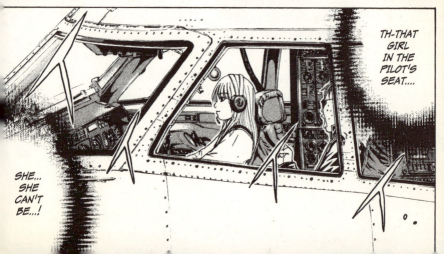

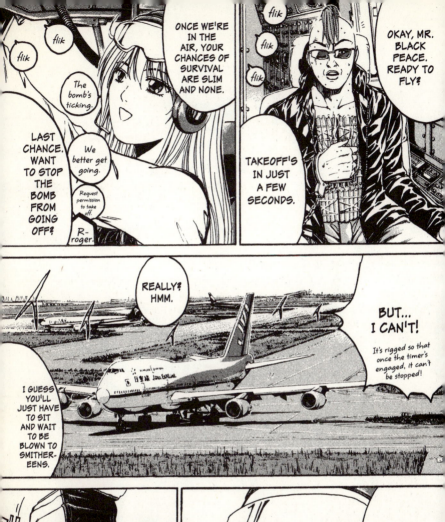

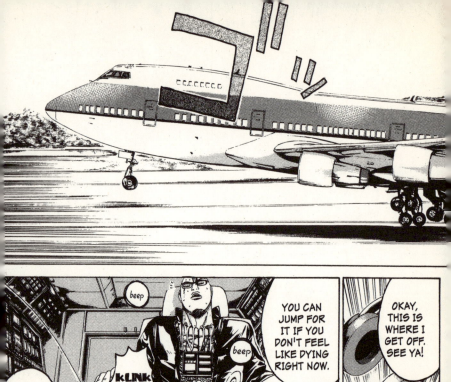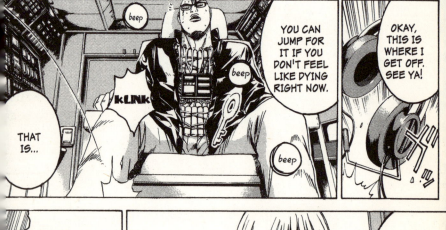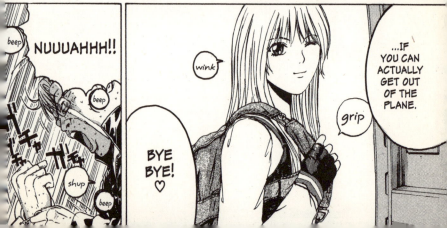

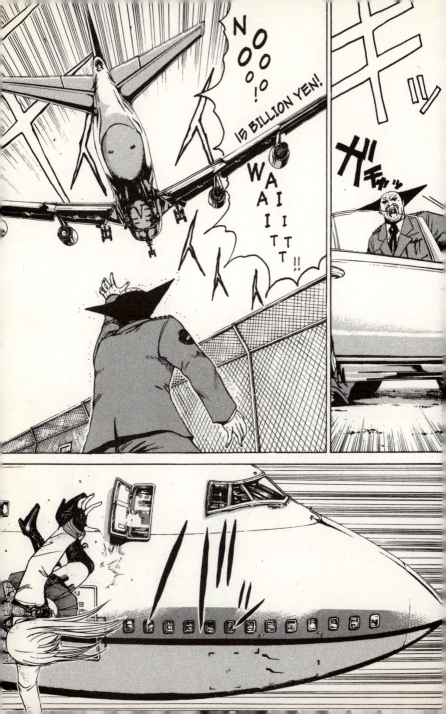

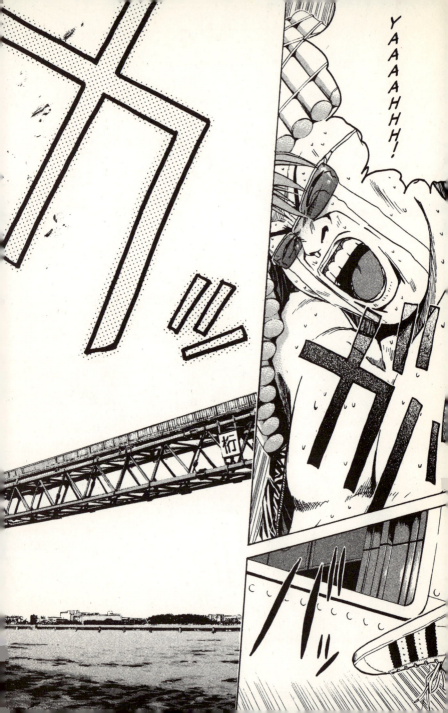

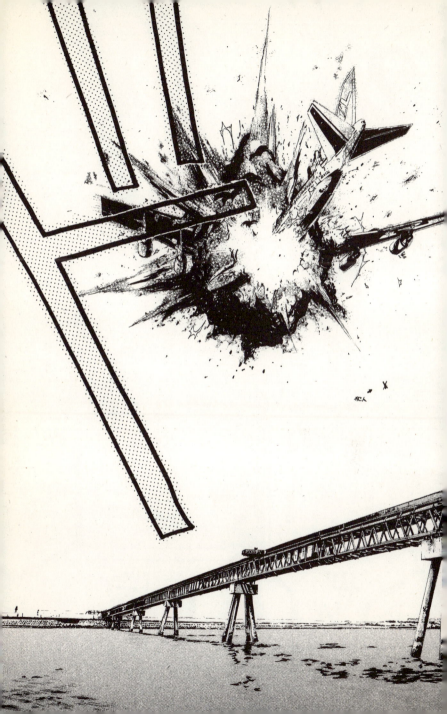

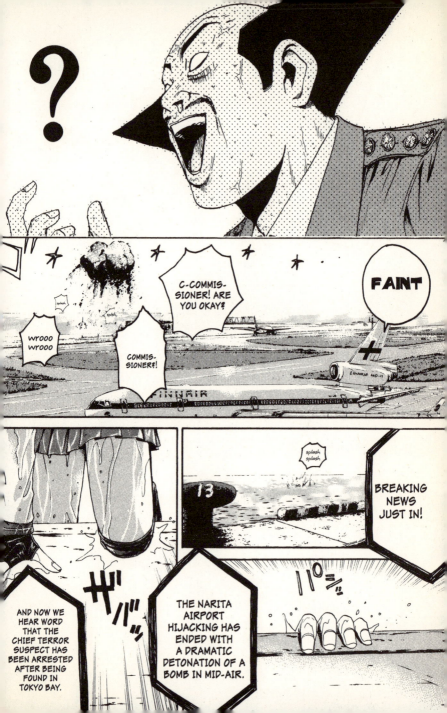

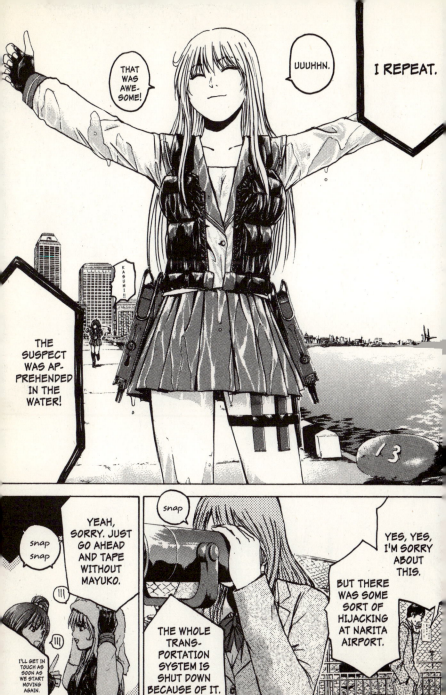

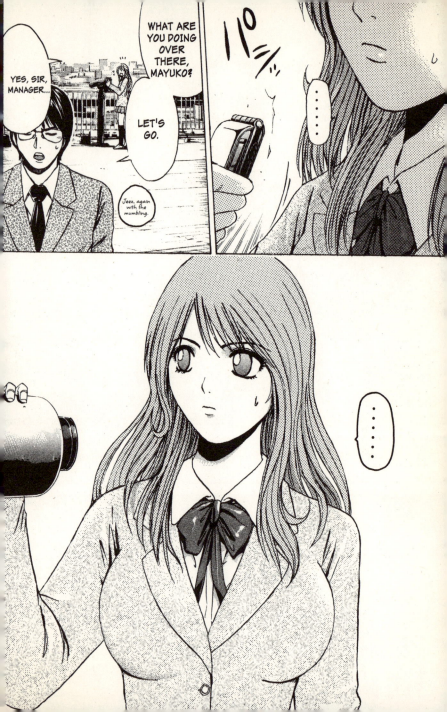

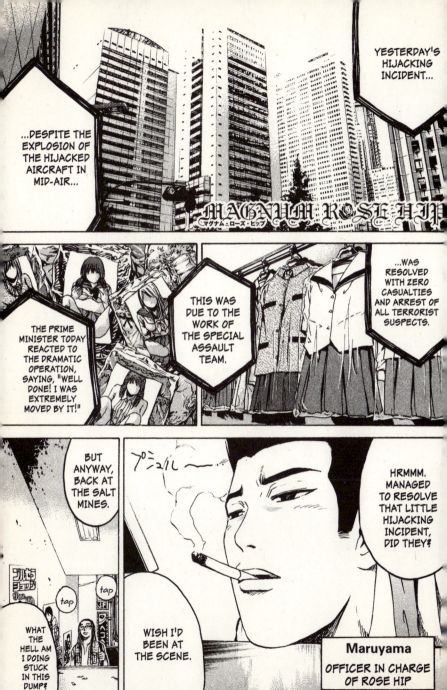

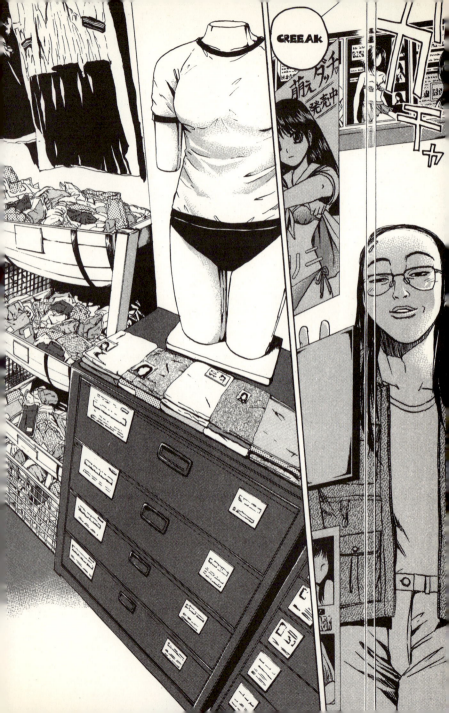

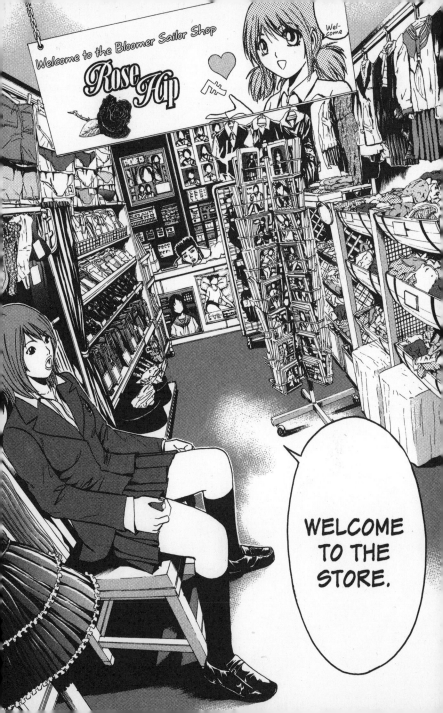

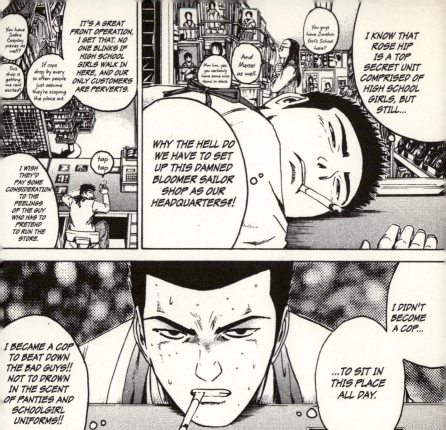

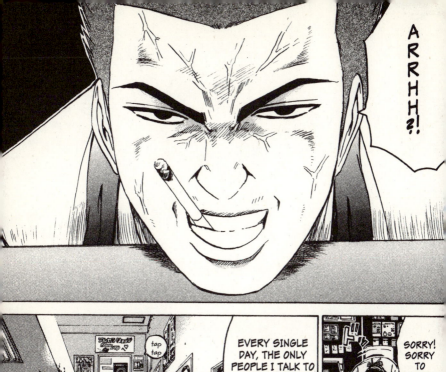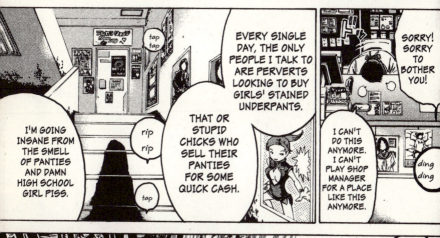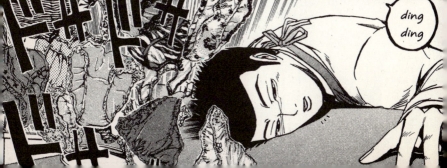

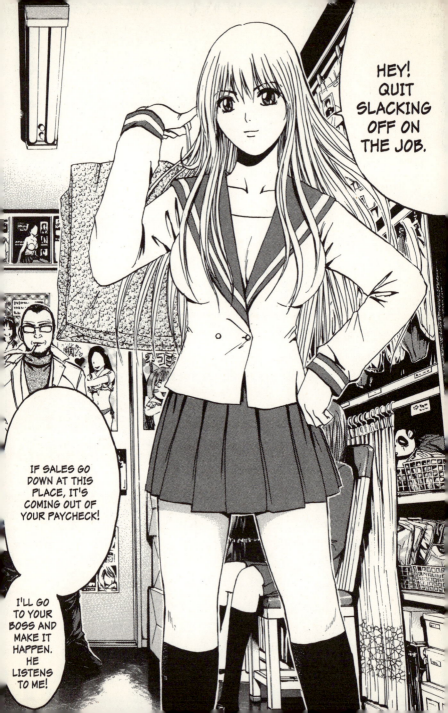

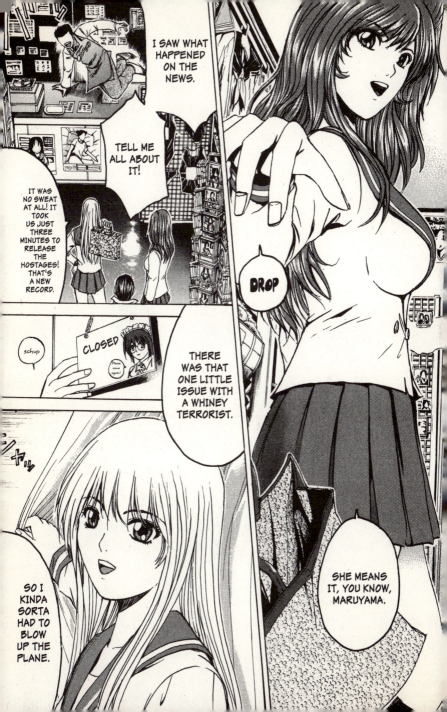

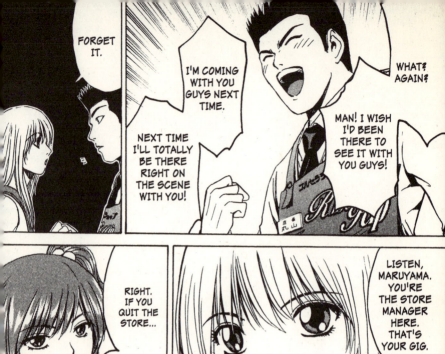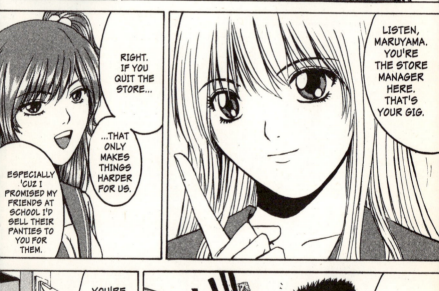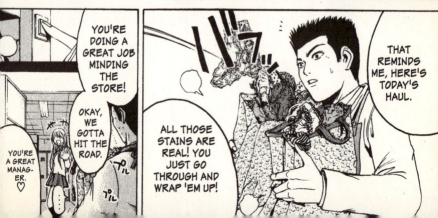

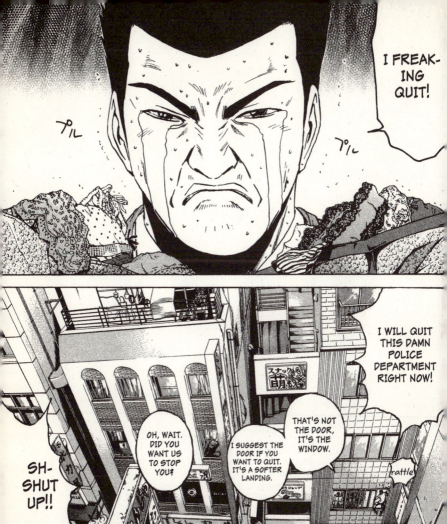

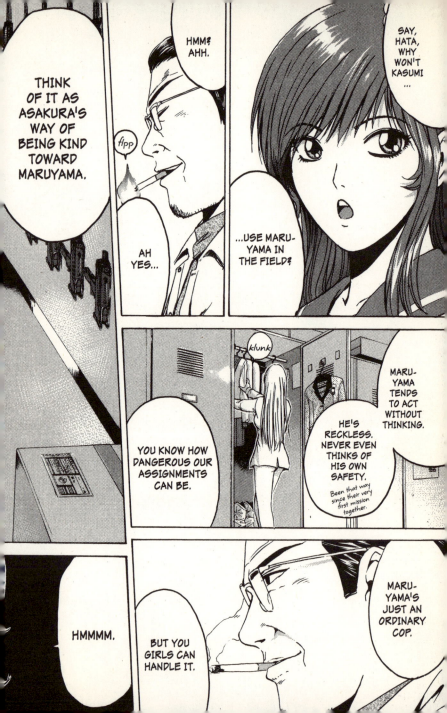

OF COURSE MARUYAMA DOESN'T SEE IT THAT WAY.

But remember, they've known each other a long time. Since before you came on the scene.

STILL, SOMETHING ABOUT THE WAY SHE TREATS HIM BUGS ME.

scrtch srtch

"Lately, well... strange men in black are following me."

"Help you?"

"Yes."

"I'm Mayuko. I just got my big break as a pop star."

"But... these people... well, they don't feel like ordinary fans."

"I don't know. I'm scared."

"My agency's been broken into, and my room as well. They turned my parents' house inside-out, too...."

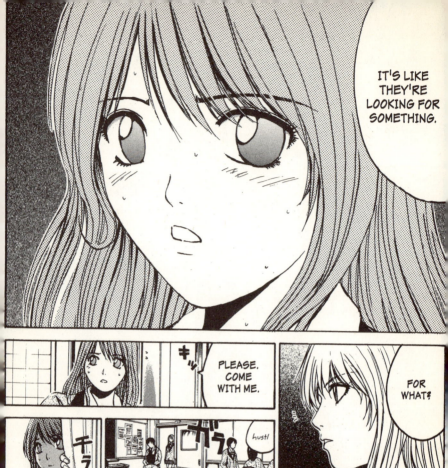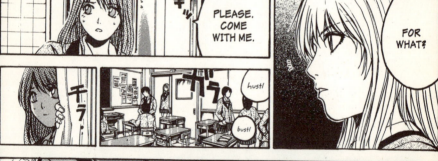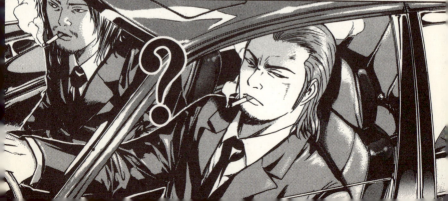

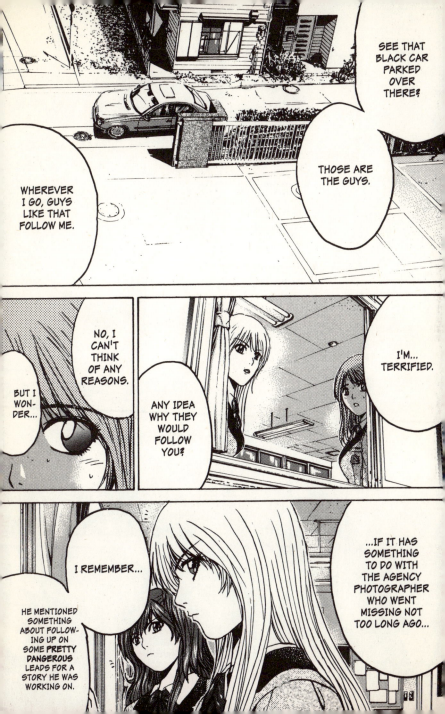

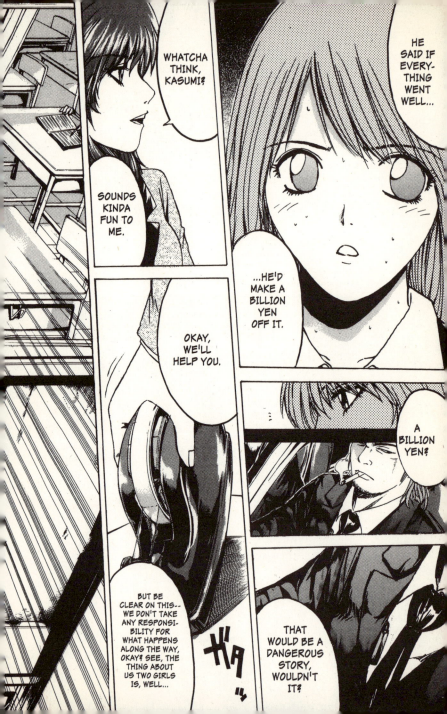

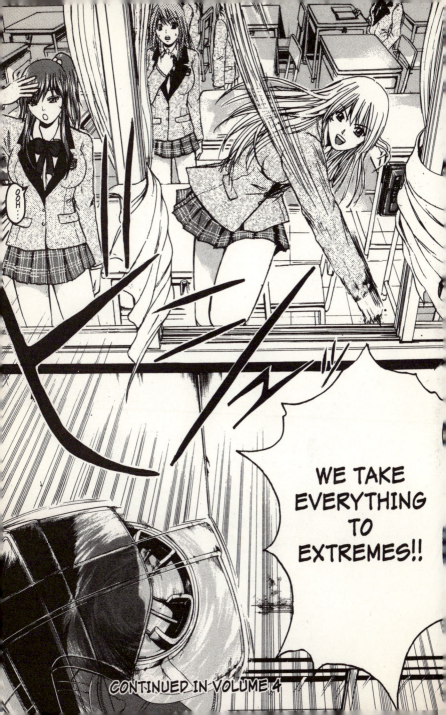

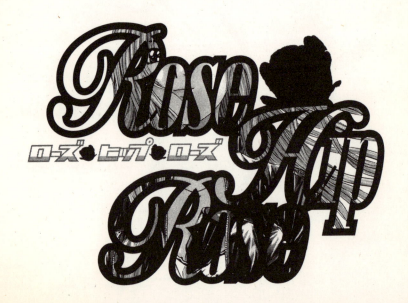

NEXT VOLUME PREVIEW

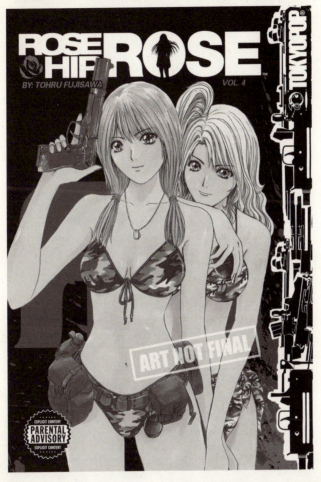

KASUMI AND NATSUKI FINALLY UNCOVER THE POWERFUL FORCE BEHIND THE MEN IN BLACK AND WHY THEY FEEL IT ABSOLUTELY NECESSARY TO SILENCE MAYUKO PERMANENTLY. THEY TRAVEL TO A DECEIVINGLY PEACEFUL NATURE PRESERVE CALLED BIRD ISLAND TO DELIVER YET ANOTHER EXPLOSIVE ENDING IN THIS FINAL VOLUME OF *ROSE HIP ROSE*.

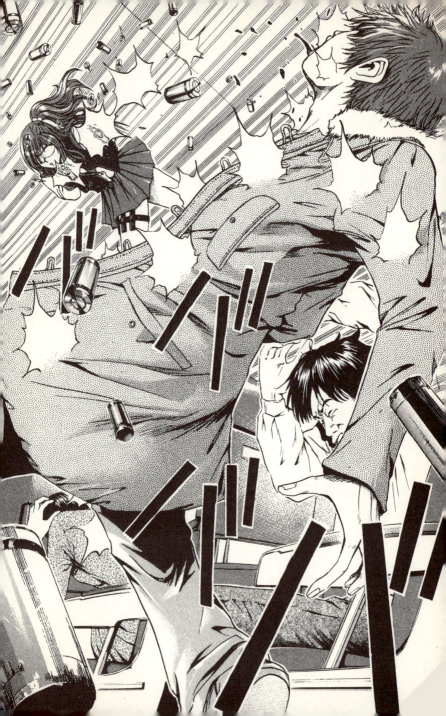

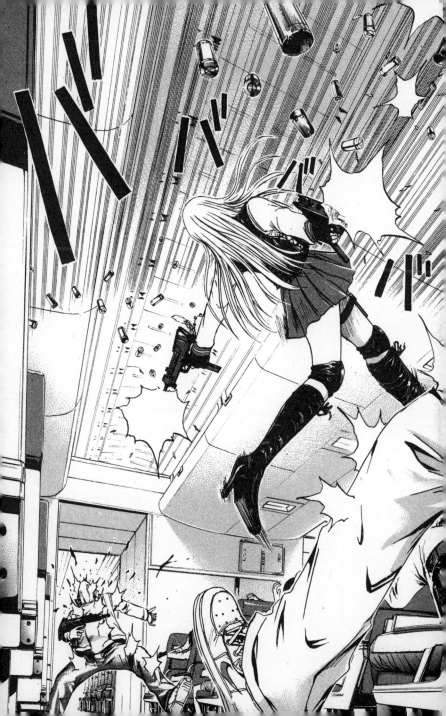

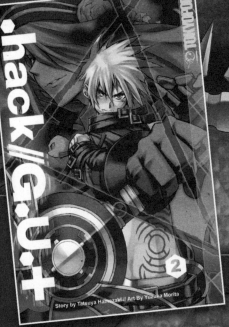

.HACK UNIVERSE

"THE WORLD" AS YOU'VE

.hack// XXXX

VOLUME 1
IN STORES JUNE 2008
© Project .hack 2002 - 2006/KADOKAWA SHOTEN

BASED ON THE HIT VIDEO GAMES!

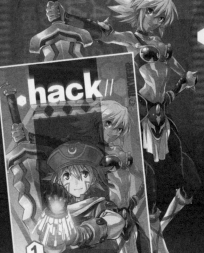

ALSO AVAILABLE:

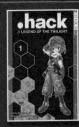

.hack//Legend of the Twilight Volumes 1-3
© 2002 Project .hack / KADOKAWA SHOTEN

HALF A MILLION COPIES SOLD!

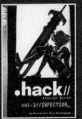

.hack// Another Birth Volumes 1-4
© 2004 MIU KAWASAKI / KADOKAWA SHOTEN

FOR MORE INFORMATION VISIT:

TOKYOPOP MANGA SUPPLEMENT

Gothic Manga based on the PS2 and Xbox Video Game!

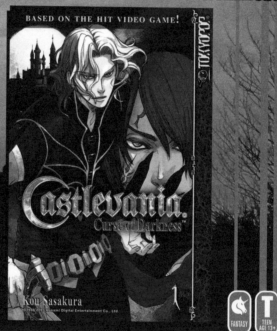

Castlevania: Curse of Darkness

A TALE OF LOYALTY, BLOODLUST AND REVENGE...

In a small village near the Romanian border, young Ted waits for his father, a mercenary in the war against Count Dracula's demon army. Little does he know that he is to become the center of a battle between two of the Count's most powerful generals...

© 2005 Kou Sasakura ©1986 2005 Konami Digital Entertainment Co., Ltd.

FOR MORE INFORMATION VISIT: WWW.TOKYOPOP.COM

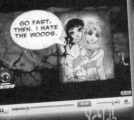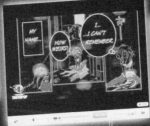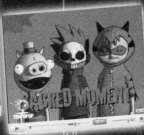

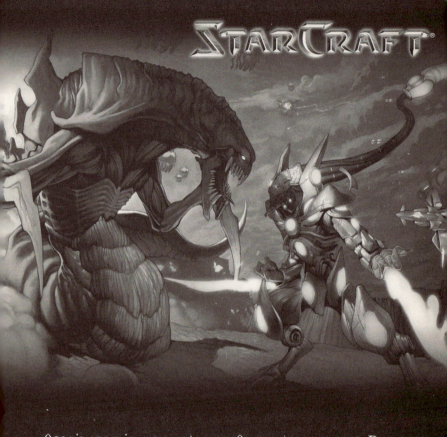

WARCRAFT: LEGENDS / STARCRAFT: FRONTLINE

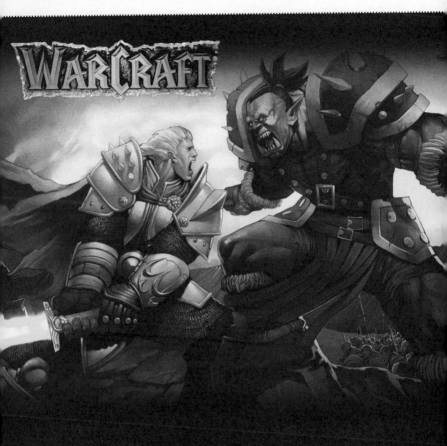

NEW MANGA BASED ON THE BESTSELLING VIDEO GAMES

Warcraft: Legends *Volume 1*

Check out www.TOKYOPOP.com/WARCRAFT
for exclusive news, updates and free downloadable art.

BUY IT AT WWW.TOKYOPOP.COM/SHOP

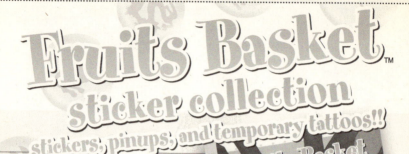

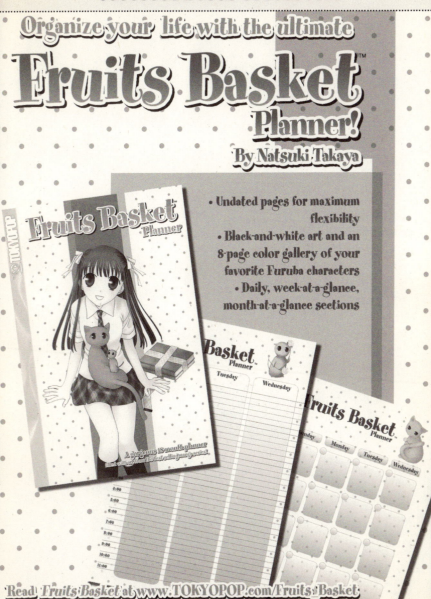

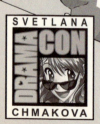

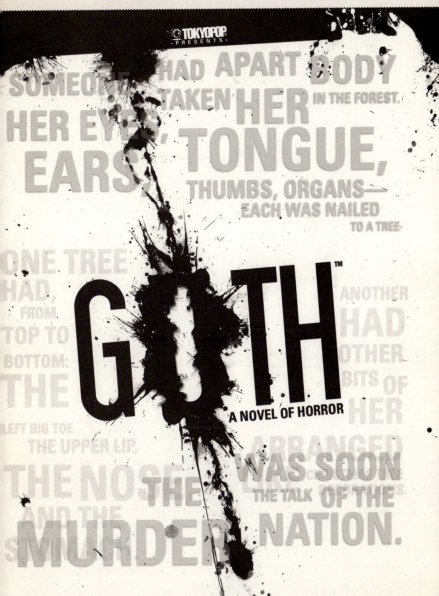

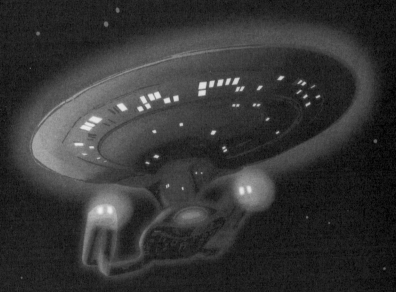